LOUISIANA SLIM
the Family

Jason Luv

With Contributions from Roger Thomas

Copyright © 2023 Jason Luv
All rights reserved
First Edition

PAGE PUBLISHING
Conneaut Lake, PA

First originally published by Page Publishing 2023

ISBN 979-8-88793-996-4 (pbk)
ISBN 979-8-88793-993-3 (digital)

Printed in the United States of America

Chapter 1

"Say, man! Do you want to f——k with this for the low or what?" asked Big Boi from Texas. "Dude, the prices are great at $16,500 a key. That's not the problem. The problem is getting the s——t back. Them highways are hot like a mutha——cka, my nigga, and if you're just going to sit back and enjoy yourself while I risk my freedom, I'm going to need you to front me whatever I buy on consignment. That way, I won't have to make extra trips on the interstate like that."

"Now I have $33,000 for two keys, but you will send me back with four. I will sell you s——t first and make the money to cover the two keys on consignment, then sell mine. So if my plan works and I know it will, I'll be buying four kilos of good coke from you plus have the money I owe you," I responded.

Big Boi looked at me as he sat in his big comfortable chair, toying with one of his new guns, then said, "Okay, I see what you're saying, and I'm willing to give you the push you need, but if you play games with my money, I will send my goons after your ass. Real talk, understand?"

I shook my head as I told him, "Fair exchange. Ain't no robbery. My word is law."

We shook hands, and I prepared for my departure.

I told Big Boi that I wanted to take the bus back instead of driving so I could concentrate on other things. He asked me if I was sure because sometimes people got caught on the buses. I told him that everything was always a fifty-fifty chance of getting caught.

I used one of the lesser known bus companies, which meant horrible conditions but was easier to blend in.

The bus was packed with people from all walks of life, either running from or toward something. I looked around as I settled into my seat. I could see the look of relief and hope overcome these passengers. They all looked like they had gone through something bad. I felt the potency of life as it permeated the air. These people were the salt of the earth, mostly Browns with only a few specks of White. I felt honored to be on this journey with them.

I landed in a seat with a pretty heavyset Mexican girl. She smiled at me and told me that this was her ticket to a new start. I asked her where she was headed. She told me just far away from Texas. She was very hopeful in her search for the elusive end of her rainbow. I asked her why she was relocating, and she said that her life in Texas was not good mainly because of hardly any money, no family, plus a bad-tempered boyfriend who liked to fight when he drank, which was often. I told her that she was doing the right thing moving as far away as she could from a situation like that. Her name was Gilda Mendez. I told her people called me Louisiana Slim, and that it was my pleasure sharing this part of the trip with her.

The poor girl had been through a lot, and the ordeal left her drained of energy because only one hour into the trip, I felt the pressure of her head leaning against my arm. I looked down at her peaceful face as I listened to her soft snoring along with the chatter of the other passengers. I reached into my pocket and pulled out my wad of cash. I peeled off twenty-five hundred, and when Gilda finally woke up, I gave her the money and told her that this was my contribution toward her fresh start.

She looked at me with tears in her eyes, thanked me, then gave me a hug. I told her that everything happens for a reason because I had decided to take the bus at the last minute. She told me that nobody had ever done anything like this for her before, and that she could never repay me. I told her that I lived a street life, and I sometimes found myself in bad situations as well, and that I believed that we were all a part of the struggle.

When it was time to get off, I gave her my number and told her to use it if she ever needed me. I wished her luck, but it was I who needed luck, toting four kilos like it was legal or something.

When I got back, I took a shower and thought about how I was going to get the money for Big Boi. I was starting off $33,000 in the red. *Well I would think about that tomorrow*, was my last thought right before my eyes closed for some much needed sleep.

The next day, I caught up with my boys and gave them the two kilos that I went and purchased for them. They were relieved that I hadn't f——cked them over by running off with their money, along with the fact that I had made it back safely. They thought I was just content with being their pack mule, but I was actually using their money to get my feet into the door with Big Boi because the truth was, I was almost broke, but I had a plan that was going to put me on top.

So to keep using their money as leverage, I told them anytime that they needed me to make a run for them, it was free of charge. They agreed without hesitation. They asked if I needed anything, but I told them I was good.

I went home and broke one kilo down into thirty-two ounces of soft. Then I contacted some friends from surrounding areas and told them that I had ounces of soft going for $1,500 apiece.

My phone was ringing off the hook. Nobody in my city knew I was making these moves. In three days, I was finished with one kilo, and I had Big Boi's money plus $15,000 of my own before I even touched the second kilo. Since it was mine to do with what I wanted, I converted it into crack.

Everyone was using the original formula, but I had a better idea.

Chapter 2

I knew that the dope that I had was the best, so that meant that I could step on it and stretch it to make more money. But instead of stretching using all kinds of impurities and knocking the potency out of it, I just put lesser grams of great dope with some baking soda and water. The result was I managed to create round cookies that looked like they weighed twenty-eight grams apiece but only contained fourteen grams apiece. We called the cookie zones.

That meant that I got seventy-two zones out of one kilo instead of the customary thirty-six, which was what everyone else everywhere was getting because this formula was widely known and used.

Now one zone of crack rock went for a thousand dollars apiece, but since I could get extra from my new formula, I could afford to sell each one at a lower cost and still make a huge profit. I decided on eight hundred apiece

When all the dealers heard that I had zones going for $200 lesser than the regular price, they bought me out in no time. So now I was sitting back with $72,600 along with the extra money I had selling Big Boi's dope for him. Now I was finally seeing my vision become a reality.

I called my boys and asked them if they would soon be ready to score again, and they told me that they would be ready in three more days.

So until they were ready, I was going to make another run using only my own money to rescore. I was transporting a little over one hundred thousand in my duffle bag. Nobody knew that I was making this run, including Big Boi. I took the bus again and was preoccupied with thoughts of my come up and how to further implement my plans. It seemed like I arrived in Texas in no time at all.

I took a taxi to Big Boi's house and rang his doorbell at three o'clock in the morning. When he answered the door and saw me standing there, his eyes lit up, and he said, "Damn, nigga! Why didn't you tell me you were coming?"

I smiled and said, "S——t! I didn't even know I was coming because it was a spur-of-the-moment decision on my part. Keeping a schedule when making runs like this is a good way to get set up for the kill, plus it reduces the chance of anyone getting in my biz, including the police. Feel me?"

"Hell yeah! Good thinking," he replied.

I saw that he was chilling, smoking on some good with his friend Mon. I joined them at his eight-foot marble table. Big Boi looked at the duffle bag, then looked at me and said, "I guess you got my money."

I smiled and said, "I got yours plus sixty-six thousand for four more keys just like I told you before I left."

He took the bag, opened it, and dumped the neatly stacked money on the table, looked up at me, and said, "That's what the f——k I'm talking about! You know, I didn't know if you would handle your biz, but not only did you keep your word, but, nigga, you also moved them four keys fast as f——k! So now I guess you want to go back with eight this time, huh?"

I told him that was the plan. He told me that he didn't have a problem with that, but he wanted me to stay an extra night so he could take me to the club to celebrate.

So the next day, we hit the mall. I bought an all Michael Jordan fit with the shoes to match. Big Boi shopped at the Versace shop. Everything was super expensive in there; plain T-shirts cost $200. For a whole fit, Big Boi spent $5,000. I only spent eight hundred.

After shopping, we headed back to Big Boi's crib to chill until it was time to go. I went into his guest room where he kept a ten-pound block of weed on a glass table for company and rolled something up. I was talking about s——t that made you cough until tears came from your eyes. This s——t was straight from Mexico.

Later on that night, we rolled out in his tricked-out, stagecoach suburban, which was painted candy blue. The big rims and the high-tech sound system made me feel like I was in a spaceship. Big Boi poured me purple codeine syrup into a bottle of Sprite cold drink, then poured the mixture into a Styrofoam glass of ice. He sipped on that while smoking on a blunt. I smoked, but I didn't sip. That s——t was way too strong, no doubt it would put me straight to sleep.

When we made it to the club, I saw a lot of tricked-out rides, but ours was a standout, reason for that was because Big Boi had a lot of clout. That clout ensured us a spot directly in front of the club. We stepped out like stars. All eyes were on us. Big Boi was known to move twenty kilos a day, of which I was a witness to the first time I was with him. That meant that niggas in the hood didn't eat unless he served them. Equally, that meant power and respect in his part of the world. We were both over six feet and five inches tall, so we looked like pro basketball players.

The club was jumping off when we entered. Everybody was bumping and grinding, dressed in the finest and freshest gear they could afford. We got a table and were served. We ordered a couple bottles of Patrón.

After my first drink, I hit the dance floor with a bad li'l shorty who was fine as hell. She had a pretty face, and she danced like she was a twerk star. When the dance was over, she followed me to our table and told Big Boi that she would show me how it goes down in the H.

He started laughing and told me that Texas girls don't play. He was already chilling with a badass Yellow Bone girl who had gold and diamonds in her mouth. We partied hard, then we got rooms at the Hilton. Shorty thought that she would show me how it goes down in the H, but I was planning on showing her how we do it in Louisiana.

Shorty was about five feet and four inches tall and weighing 110 pounds all in the right places. As soon as we entered the room, we started undressing while we kissed. I sat at the edge of the bed while she got on top, straddling me. As soon as I entered her hot depths, she gasped, locked her arms around my neck and her legs around my waist. I stood up as I impaled her with my ten inches. Positioning one hand at the bottom of her soft juicy ass and the other at the base of her neck for support, I rammed my angry d——k into her small tunnel with monster strokes. She was trapped and had no choice but to endure the pleasure of pain I was inflicting on her. Yeah, Louisiana s——t.

Shorty was in heaven. When I finally bust, we collapsed on the bed, laughing. Shorty looked at me and said, "Damn! Country boys go hard as f——k! Now you know I will want some of that whenever you're in town on business, so I'm giving you an unlimited p——ssy coupon." That statement had us both laughing. Shorty was fun to be around. Her real name was Adriene, and she was superhot to the touch. We exchanged numbers the next day when I paid for a taxi to bring her and the other girl home.

Chapter 3

I dressed down for my trip back home in old work pants and an oily shirt. With all the dope I was transporting, I had to be as inconspicuous as possible. At a glance, I appeared to be broke and struggling. I drove no more than five miles over the speed limit, being very careful and alert. I had way too much product to try and run with if I got pulled over, so my driving had to be on point.

When I finally reached my home state, I felt a huge sense of relief. When I hit the hood, it was good to see all the smiling faces on everybody who were walking around in the shinning sun doing their thing.

I pulled up to a corner store to grab a pack of cigs and a cold beer. As I stepped out of the store, I took a swig of my beer. My cell phone went off. It was one of the guys whom I had made that first life-changing run for. Money Mike asked me if I was ready to make another trip for them. I told him that I would holler back in about an hour.

I smiled to myself because these boys still thought I was just their runner, but actually, they were both two of my main clienteles. But as long as they thought that I was beneath them, I could fly under the radar.

I made it to my stash spot, unloaded my product, then went out to meet them. When I pulled up, they were all smiles. They wanted three keys this time. They put their money together and gave it to me. They told me that they were splitting the difference on one of the keys. Mike told me that the total amount in the bag was fifty thousand plus an extra five hundred for my expenses. I told them cool, and that I would leave for Texas that night. We shook hand, then I left.

Things were going according to my plan. I wasn't back home a full day and already had fifty of the sixty-six thousand that I owed Big Boi.

I went back home and put fifty g's in my stash spot and grabbed two keys. I had all my paraphernalia to cook it up in my bag along with my gun. I jumped into my car and casually laid the bag on the front seat. I headed out to the country to the sparsely furnished old house that I rented. I always felt safe here. It was off the grid because no one knew about it. It was a lonely old house far from the road, and the closest neighbor was a mile away on either side. If anyone tried to tip down on me, I would spot them coming with no problem. The ideal place to do dirt. I decided to whip both keys into one hundred and forty-four fourteen gram plates.

I worked feverishly until I completed the task. When I finally had each zones individually wrapped in plastic, I loaded them into my bag. Selling a quick thirty-six zones to my out-of-town buyers netted me $28,800.

Now I was good on what I owed plus twelve thousand for myself. So I called Money Mike when I got home. He picked up and asked, "What it do?"

I said, "Yo, I'm calling to tell y'all that Big Boi said that all his keys have been converted into zones. So his question is, do you still want to score?"

They said "yes, it was all good."

I told them that I would have their package ready for them in the morning. They told me to be careful and make it back safe.

Life is crazy; just last month, I was breaking down one zone into fifty-two rocks and chasing cars down, trying to make a sale. I used to get it the hard way in the sun, rain, sleet, or snow. Now I had six kilos and $18,000 of my own. I f——cking love America! I still remained in the shadows because safety came first.

I went over to one of my lady friends to kick it with her. Valencia was very beautiful and very book smart. She didn't know much about the streets, and I liked that.

We always had fun together. Valencia was still in college but was home for the summer. "What's up, Val?" I asked as I hugged and kissed her.

She pulled back, smiled, and said, "So you finally made time to come and see me, huh?"

I told her that her body was calling me as I squeezed her soft round ass.

We started undressing and then attacked each other. We were both super athletic, which propelled us to go at it hard and fast. After we were both spent, we laid back on her couch and talked.

I told her that one day I was going to leave the streets, then marry her.

She kissed me, then said, "Slim, you always talk the good talk, but you will never leave those streets because that would be the same as a fish trying to live out of water. But I hope you know that you can't hustle forever."

I told her that I was working on a plan that would reposition my current place in the streets, allowing myself more time to accomplish bigger things.

"That sounds great. I will keep my fingers crossed," she replied as her nimble fingers went down and placed me inside her for round two.

When I left Val's place, I went and delivered the zones to Chrisville and Money Mike. When I opened my duffle bag and emptied the zones on their table, they both yelled, "F——k yeah!"

Chapter 4

"Damn, Slim, you don't play. Was it harder to bring all this back in zones instead of just three smaller-sized keys of powder?" asked Chrisville.

I told him that I was good on bringing it back either way. Money Mike said that getting it already cooked saved them time because they could hit the streets directly plus never have to worry about a manufacturing charge. I told them that they couldn't lose f——cking with me.

When I got up to leave, I told them that Big Boi said if they paid an extra two thousand a key, they could receive their shipment the same day.

"Wow! That way, we would never run out of dope. We're down to pay extra for that type of service," said Chrisville.

Money Mike asked if the transactions were still going to be going through me, and I told them yes because the plug wasn't trying to meet new people.

Now I went home and transferred all my money and coke to my house in the country. I spent the night there and woke up early, jamming some gangster rap. I planned on cooking four keys so I could have them on deck ready for distribution. My goal was to have four hundred and eighty-eight zones by the end of the day. S——t, I was operating three microwaves at one time, putting mad work in.

Total concentration and all I could see was dollar signs. The whole time I worked, my mind was churning with plans to monopolize the drug trade in my section, and it became obvious to me that

I would have to regulate the prices. I had enough product to do that because everything from here on out was profit for me.

I finished cooking and packaging twelve hours later. It was time to put some people to work, but that could wait until next week. For now, it was time to build my capital, so I made some calls. I told some of my contacts that I knew a guy who was willing to sell zones for a measly five hundred a piece. When they heard this, I immediately got sales for seventy-two of them.

I got everything together, grabbed my gun, and took off to make the drops. Everything went smoothly, and I returned home with thirty-six thousand to add to the eighteen I already had stashed.

I decided that after I got off one more key, I would make a trip to rescore. Two days later, I moved a hundred more. Armed with Big Boi's sixty-six plus one hundred and four thousand of my own money, I departed for Texas at midnight that night.

This was a very important trip, so I hoped everything would go right. I arrived at my plug's house at four o'clock that morning. He answered his door, holding a nine-millimeter handgun. He smiled when he saw me and said, "Louisiana Slim! My main man, come on in."

I walked in and asked if he was alone, and he told me that he had a couple of b——ches in his room. I threw my duffle bag on the table and told him I was ready to handle biz now because I wanted to be back on the road ASAP. His response was, "Damn, li'l nigga, what's the rush? Ain't you tired from all that driving?"

I told him that I was good then sat down and counted out the sixty-six thousand that I owed him. He just smiled. Then I counted out ninety-nine more thousands for six more keys. He looked at me and said, "Man, you move dope faster than anyone I know."

He took the money into his room and came back with twelve keys. I looked at the product, then told him that I wasn't there to get anything fronted but just to score the six. He asked me if I was sure. I told him I appreciated his help, but now I was good. I also told him that from here on out, he could expect to serve me for a hundred thousand or better every trip I would make.

He told me that he respected that, but that if I ever needed anything fronted to me in the future, I could get it just off my world because now he knew my word was law. I thanked him, loaded up the six bricks, shook his hand and then burned off. Instead of driving back, I rented a room and got some sleep.

I hit the road early the next morning and drove straight home. With over ten bricks of coke in my inventory, I was ready to start shaking and baking like I wanted to. I had my cell turned off for the entire trip, and now that it was back on, I was getting hit up left and right. Chrisville and Money Mike had fifty-two thousand for a hundred zones—well a hundred and eight to be exact.

I went and got their money and told them that they would have their product in an hour's time. When I finally arrived, they were both ecstatic. Chrisville said, "Slim man, we will get rich f——cking with you, homie."

I told them that Big Boi was impressed with how fast they were moving their product, and on the strength of me, he was now willing to match whatever they bought on consignment, if they were about that life.

They both said that it wouldn't be a problem but would need a little more time in between them to rescore. I told them that I would holler at him and see what was up. Money Mike looked at me and asked, "Slim, why you ain't asking your plug to front you some product?"

I said, "Man, y'all know that I don't have that kind of clientele to move s——t like that. Besides, Big Boi pays me cash money for every trip that I make for him."

Chrisville said, "Nigga, I knew you were getting broke off some kind of way." He started laughing.

I punched him on the arm and said, "Not the kind of big money y'all niggas be getting."

We all laughed as I burnt off.

When I got home, I called them back and told them that the plug said it was all good, and that I would get the other one hundred and eight zones to them later on that day.

JASON LUV

    I served my boys from out of town with the last hundred zones for the same low price of five hundred apiece. I now had one hundred thousand of cold hard cash of my own plus six more kilos. It was almost time.

Chapter 5

I chilled out at my spot in the country and cooked up my standard four hundred and eighty-eight zones.

It was time for me to find myself some workers. I had special criteria in mind for my selection of anyone who I was going to add to my team: one was the ability to follow orders, two was staying out of dumb s———t, and three was ultimate loyalty.

I rolled through a few hoods that I was familiar with and observed the little hustlers.

I saw this youngster named Tugga and told him to jump into the car with me, which he did. "What's been up with you?" I asked.

"Man, same ole s———t. My mom and stepdad are tripping on me for nothing. I'm the only one they treat that way. They have no love for a nigga," he retorted.

"So why don't you get your own place?" I asked.

"S———t! With hardly no product, I can only make a few dollars here and there," he responded.

I passed him some of that good I was smoking on and picked up three more hustlers, who were doing bad. Their names were Lil "G", Rambeezy, and a girl they called Teela. I took them to my house and offered them a beer as they sat and waited. I could tell that they were all confused especially being in my home for the first time.

I looked them all in the eyes and began talking. "I got you all here today because of all the niggas out there, I dig your style the most. I think you four could come up in the game if you had the right nigga behind you, and guess what? I'm that nigga.

Now for me to shake you niggas back and put y'all where you need to be, I'm going to require some things on your part."

After I told them the criteria, I asked, "Are you niggas hopping on the money train?"

They all agreed, and I began to tell them my plan. I told them that we were about to take over the streets. I looked at Tugga and asked how much the zones cost in his part of the hood. He told me anywhere from eight to a thousand. They all told me that it was the same everywhere.

I told them, "Cool. Because the nigga with the best prices move the most dope. So with that in mind, we are about to regulate the prices and sale zones for only four hundred apiece for a couple of weeks. We will have everybody and their mommas looking to score from y'all, trying to get some good snow at this bargain basement price.

"Now to achieve the goal that I've set, I will have to lose money first, but in the end, we will win big."

I went into my room and came back with four duffle bags. I threw one at each person's feet and said, "Okay, these bags are what I call your balling kits. Inside each one, you will find twenty-five zones, a cell phone, a gun, and $5,000 in cash. For every twenty-five that you sell, you will be paid $5,000. So at the price that I've set, you each owe ten thousand. Do not sell a zone for anything higher than the set price, and yes, I know that I'm giving dope away for now.

"The idea is to make sure that everybody in the streets eat and get their money up, and since you four will be the cause of it, they will respect you and be grateful."

I told everyone that didn't have their own place to get one. "Okay, I don't want anyone knowing that I'm the new plug, so never discuss business with me unless it's on the throwaway phones that I've given y'all."

Everybody got up to leave, and each one of them gave me a hug. They expressed their thanks for me letting them get on the money train.

Chrisville and Money Mike hit me up and told me that they had the plug's money plus wanted the same deal. I told them I would be there shortly to pick up the money, and I would holler at Big Boi before I left for the pickup.

When I got to their spot, I gave them two hundred and sixteen zones, and they gave me $108,000. My capital was growing exponentially.

My life seemed to be moving with a purpose. I was changing the landscape of my reality by use of mental manipulation and the comprehensive nature of understanding the economic struggle poverty inflicts on some. Was I doing it in the most moralistic way imagined? Of course not, but my reasoning was that sometimes you have to do a little bad to do a little good, strategically speaking, especially if you came from nothing.

The streets nicknamed getting money *eating*, and I was going to make sure that people who didn't get fed in the past would now have full stomachs. Would I ever come out of the shadows? Yes, I think that fact was inevitable from the start of my operation. How else would I accomplish most of my goals? But for now, part of my blueprint included me remaining unseen.

I made some calls to my out of towners and sold seventy-two zones, adding another thirty thousand to my bankroll. With only a hundred zones left ready distribution, I decided to cook the last two kilos, which would boost my inventory to two hundred and forty zones.

I now had over a quarter of a million in cash, with another hundred thousand expected from Chrisville and Mike upon their rescoring, plus another forty thousand from my new crew.

It would soon be time to make another run across the state line. Most likely, Big Boi was wondering what was happening with me. At the moment, I had enough money to score fifteen keys, but I decided that I would let my people bring in what they owed, then drop what was left of my inventory on them and get twenty keys instead.

Well I didn't have to wait long; my crew finished up and were given twenty-five more zones. Chrisville and Mike finished a few days later and brought the fifty-four thousand plus another fifty to re-up. I told them that Big Boi said they would have to wait a couple of weeks to get more on consignment. They said it was cool with them.

Big Boi, here I come.

Chapter 6

Three hundred and forty thousand dollars were a lot of money to be taking a chance on the highway with, but "no nuts, no glory" was the name of the game.

I grabbed my balling kit and took off. I kept my duffle bag on the floor on the passenger side of my car. I put it there just in case something went wrong. I truly hoped that I wouldn't get pulled over because I was willing to shoot it out with any cop who was unfortunate and got in my way. But luck was still a constant companion of mine and enabled my arriving safely at Big Boi's house.

I hit Big Boi on his cell. When he answered, he said, "Slim! What's up, baby?"

"Open your door, Big Boi. I'm in front of your door," I responded.

Sounds of his laughter were heard before he opened his door. "Man, you move like a ghost, my nigga. Come on," he said as he placed his big arm around my shoulder, guiding me into his house.

I threw my two bags on his big marble table. He looked at the bags with wide eyes and said, "I thought that you was on some chill s———t, but, damn, nigga, you been getting it, huh?"

"Yeah, I've been doing a little something. I had to put a crew together to help me move my product more efficiently, which is why it took me a little longer to make my way here. I had to get everything ironed out," I retorted.

"Good, because that means business is looking real nice for you. So what are you trying to cop this time?" he asked.

"Well I decided to go hard or go home, so I'm here to get twenty kilos this time. I have three hundred and forty thousand for you," I said.

"Damn! Nigga, you on some next level s——t, huh? Well you know I got you. I assume you're hitting the highway again tonight, so let me grab that for you," he replied.

When he came back with the dope, he said, "Listen, I admire the way you've put down your hustle, so I threw an extra five, on the house."

I shook my head in approval and asked him if he was ready to count the money. He replied, saying, "Nah, I trust you. Go ahead and get out of here. You know time is money."

We shook hands, and I left. This time, I drove straight home. I was anxious to make it back home because all I was thinking were money and power.

When I finally made it back, I headed to my spot in the country. I threw my bag next to my sofa and then flopped down on it, exhausted. I went to sleep.

I woke up the next morning, showered, ate something, then turned my cell on. I saw a lot of missed calls. My crew had first priority, so I called them and told them to meet me at my house in thirty minutes.

Then I called Chrisville and Money Mike. I asked them if they had that change for Big Boi that was missing on the last exchange. Chrisville laughed and said, "Nigga, I thought we had got away with murder."

I laughed and said, "Big Boi knows his number."

They told me to swing by and pick it up.

When I finally made it home, my crew was chilling in my yard. I got down and went and greeted everybody with a hug and a handshake. When we were all seated inside the house, they told me that they were finished moving the product they had. When they tried to give me the money, I told them I was proud of them, and that I wanted them to keep the money because a drought was about to kick in for a couple of weeks, and that the extra ten thou apiece was to be used by them to ride it out.

LOUISIANA SLIM THE FAMILY

They were all surprised. Tugga said, "Damn, Uncle Slim, nobody never done nothing like this for me my whole life! When you f——cks with a nigga, you really f——cks with a nigga."

They were all nodding their heads in agreement.

I smiled, got up, and passed everybody five more grand apiece as I said, "S——t, all you niggas gotta do is follow orders, and y'all will never have money worries f——cking with me."

Teela asked me what the extra money was for, and I told them it was for moving the twenty-five zones and because following orders gets a nigga paid.

"Now, Tugga, I want you to go and buy yourself a li'l used car so you can move around better, and swing by your mom's house and give her a couple of racks to help her pay her bills," I told him.

I took the rest of them to my favorite Mexican restaurant. We were all laughing and joking when the tiny Mexican waitress appeared in front of us and took our orders. After she did so, thirty minutes later, we were all licking our fingers; the food was so good. I looked at them and said, "My plans for y'all have changed because I need a lot of things done simultaneously sometimes, and y'all selling zones for me is not top priority."

"We're not out of work, are we?" asked Ram.

"No, now you guys work full time, on call, and in any capacity that I need. If I give you an order, don't hesitate to follow it. For example, Ram, if I tell you to blow a nigga's brain's out, do it. That goes for the rest of y'all. We are about to be the heart of these streets, and if you can't f——k with it, get up and leave now."

I looked at Teela and asked, "Are you scared to bust your gun?"

"F——k no! If you call a shot, I will do what you say point blank. S——t, because of you, I'm looking good and smelling good, and I'm able to look out for my family. Everyone here should feel the same, so we're down for whatever," she hit back.

"Yeah, Slim, we were already talking about riding for you if something went down," replied li'l "G."

"It's all good then. Now I'm taking y'all somewhere else, but before we leave, I want everybody to leave a hundred dollar tip for our waitress."

Everyone did so, and when she saw her tip, she started crying. She thanked us and gave us each a hug.

When we got outside, I told them that we would be doing a lot of good like we had just done for our waitress, but we would have to get our hands dirty, and that we couldn't rise to the top otherwise because everyone knew the dope game was a dirty one.

Chapter 7

Our next stop was at the corner store, which was owned by Adam the Arab. When we got inside, I told Adam that me and my crew needed to holler at him in private. I had my trusty duffle bag with the fifty thou from Chrisville and Money Mike.

Adam led us into his private building adjacent to his store and asked what was it that we needed. I told him that I needed some guns, big and small. I told him that I had fifty racks to spend. He smiled and said, "Ah, business must be good if you're spending that kind of cash. Obviously, you need to protect yourselves and your investments, I presume. Well I got some great high quality artillery for you."

He showed me a few AR-15s, Glocks, Berettas, and big revolvers. My crew were all impressed with his inventory. Adam said, "Slim, for another twenty, I got you plenty of ammunition and some night vision goggles to go with your purchase."

I told him that I would go get another forty thousand if he had silencers too.

"Damn. Are you planning on going to war with somebody!" he exclaimed and laughed.

I told him preparation was always a good move. He told me to go and get the rest of the money while he got everything together for my crew. I went to my stash spot and returned twenty minutes later. After biz was concluded, we headed to my house.

"Damn! Unc, we are strapped like a mutha——cka," said Rambeezy.

Teela smiled and said, "Yeah, ain't nobody around here on our level right now. We just moved to the top of the food chain."

"That's the idea," I told them. "Everything is going according to plan. Now y'all can bust out and go and chill for a couple of weeks, then we will be back in motion."

They grabbed their money out of the closet, but as they started to leave, I told Teela to stay put.

When the boys were gone, Teela walked up to me, giggling and sticking her hand under my shirt, and said, "Let me guess, you want to sample my goods and see what I'm working, huh?"

As I bent down and kissed her, I smiled and said, "Wouldn't be a good business man if I didn't know the quality of my product."

She met my kiss with a fevered pitch as I peeled her clothes off and placed her on my couch. Her skin was a delicious caramel color, and she was fine as hell. I hit her p——ssy hard and fast with her matching my intensity. At one point, when I was deep inside of her, she reached up, held me tight, and whispered into my ear, "Slim, this p——ssy is yours, and I'm down to do whatever you want, no questions asked."

At that moment, I bust inside of her smoldering heat and said, "Good!"

After we were both dressed, we discussed business. I began telling her that sometimes I was going to send her on missions and special assignments, and that she was going to be my second-in-command.

"I'm up for it," she replied.

I got up and got twenty more thousand to add to her bankroll and ordered her to go shopping for provocative clothing. I told her that I needed her to be sexually alluring and dangerous if she was to be my second-in-command, and that I was going to cop her a drop-top Benz as part of her new image.

She kissed me and said, "That's what's up."

Before she left, I told her not to get intimate with me in front of the boys, and that whatever they thought and what they actually knew were two different things. She told me that she understood. I also told her to be on the lookout for at least five more members to add to our squad, preferably those who knew how to handle a gun.

She told me to consider it done. I told her that I was tempted to hit the p——ssy again, but I had too much I had to do. She smiled and said, "Well, just add a few pit stops while you're running laps around these niggas."

Now I had to go back to the country and cook up some more dope, and I meant a s——tload this time. I was going to work for a week straight. Because of the drought that I was about to enforce, niggas would get desperate and be willing to pay whatever price that I would set, and when that happens, my inventory had to be full tilt. I was going to make my first million, imagine that. I called myself the skinny, hungry nigga, so I had to eat some more. LOL. I planned to cook 1,426 zones or a little more. Then I was going to drive the prices up to $1,200 a zone and make a king's ransom.

*****

Meanwhile, back on the cut, Chrisville and Money Mike were in deep conversation.

"Say, man, that nigga Louisiana Slim is the dumbest mutha——cka on the planet. I don't think he understands how much money we're making because of him," Chrisville told Mike.

Money Mike laughed and said, "Yeah, he's a duck-ass nigga, but I wish that Big Boi, whoever he is, would do business directly instead of going through Slim because I don't like a nigga having that kind of power over me. But since Big Boi is paying him for the transaction, it's not hurting us. Say, let's call Slim and tell him to come and get them ends for Big Boi."

Chrisville took out his hitter and dialed.

*****

I picked up on the third ring and asked, "What it do?"

Chrisville told me they had the money for Big Boi. I grabbed my keys and bounced to make the pickup. I needed that cash to hold me over for the drought.

When I got there, I told them that I was there to get only what they owed but nothing else because Big Boi said it would be a couple of days before the next shipment came in.

"F——k!" yelled Mike. "We will miss out on a lot of money waiting like that, but I guess we ain't got no choice. Slim, tell him that we will be ready to score as soon as he's straight," said Mike.

I grabbed the fifty K they owed and bailed out, turning my cell off. I was headed to the country to work my wrist.

Eight days later, I was done cooking and packaging two thousand zones. I finally turned my phone back on to find a slew of missed calls. Chrisville and Mike had tried over a dozen times to contact me. I called them back, and Chrisville cried out in exasperation, "Slim man, what's up, baby? Is Big Boi ready to do some business or what?"

Chapter 8

I told Chrisville that it was over because Big Boi got popped. "Man, them fed boys ran in his spot. F——k, I almost got caught up over there, but luckily, he had sent me on a run for him. Then he called me from jail and told me to go and pick his bread up from a few niggas and bring it to his people so they could bond him out," I said.

"Damn! That's f——cked up. Now what are we going to do? Them fiends are going crazy without dope in the streets," replied Chrisville.

"Big Boi is out of commission because the laws will be watching his every move once he's out, so I'm not going back that way ever because I'm not trying to take a jailhouse vacation. But I have a friend who's plugged in with a boss b——tch by the name of Teela. Now I don't know if he can plug me in with her, but I will see what I can do. If it's good, I will get back at y'all, but if not, then it was fun while it lasted," I retorted.

"Okay, my nigga, see what you can do because s——t is real out here. Just holla back," he responded and hung up.

I laughed my ass off when I hung up. Then I called Teela and ordered her to come to my house.

She was knocking on my door twenty minutes later.

"What it do, Slim?" she asked.

"Let's go cop you that Benz because you are about to become the head b——tch in charge," I said and laughed.

She looked at me with confusion in her eyes, but I told her I would explain everything after we got her new ride. She was all smiles as we looked at all the stylish cars. I wanted something eye catching, so I picked out an all-black drop-top with caramel guts to match her skin color. She was already dressed in designer clothing, so she looked absolutely gorgeous in her new sports car. I paid $75,000 for the joint.

Business concluded, I told her to meet me at our favorite Mexican restaurant. When we were finally seated, I called the rest of the crew to join us.

Teela looked at me in the eyes and asked, "What's going down?"

I told her that the drought was about to be over in a few days, and she was going to play the part of the new plug for me. I gave her the rundown of her new job. She nodded her head in understanding as I revealed my plan to her. I also told her that I was going to buy a house the following week for the crew to live in because whenever she would go out, they would be going with her, especially club appearances because we were making a statement for the streets, and that statement was that Mrs. Teela was running s——t now.

"Damn! I feel like I'm dreaming, but when I look outside and see my new Benz, I know s——t is real. You already know that I'm down for whatever. Oh, I got them other five new niggas ready to join the family. I even took them out to the shooting range, and they are official," she replied.

"That's good because I will need them to get on the grind for me. Are they hungry?" I asked.

"S——t, them boys are starving. I handpicked them myself," she hit back.

I nodded my head in approval.

I looked up to see Tugga and Ram walked through the doors, heading toward our table. When they sat down, Ram said, "Damn! Did y'all see that clean ass Benz parked outside? That's the new I-8 Benz, huh?"

Teela said, "Yeah, that's the new I-8 point, and it belongs to your boss."

They looked at me, and Lil "G" said, "Wow, Slim, that's how you're coming."

I smiled, looked at them, and said, "Nah, it's Teela's car. She will be head of operations from here on out, so if she gives you an order, follow it and protect her with your lives. Understand?"

They all nodded.

I told them of my plans, and that I would always be the one calling shots. Tugga said, "Slim, you are one shrewd nigga."

I smiled and said, "This is chess, not checkers, mutha——cka!"

We all started laughing.

I revealed the house-buying decision, then sent them out to go and buy an all-black SUV for them to mob in whenever Teela had to make a move. I expressed to them that this was a serious game that we were playing because it was the ultimate game, and that I was planning on us winning at all cost. I also told them that Teela was going to make her debut that weekend with the whole crew in tow, and that Lil "G" was to be the moving piece in the club who would introduce me to Teela. I told everyone to make sure they were all strapped.

When the boys left, I told Teela that she was to let the new members know that they were going to be moving fifty zones apiece at a time. Before she got up, I handed her the keys to my car and told her to go and get her other car from my house and to just place my keys under the floor mat. I told her that I was going to stash her Benz until she made her debut. I kissed her, gave her a hug, then whispered in her ear, "This is your world, baby."

She shook her head in confirmation and sauntered out of the restaurant with the sound of her expensive high heels clicking on the floor.

I jumped in the Benz and headed out to the country. I was going to make over two million on the two thousand zones.

Now what I needed were some cookers because I had too much product to do it on my own, and I needed a new place to do the cooking. It would have to be a very remote spot. I still had another twelve kilos. Well I would think about that later. What was on my mind was, *Could Big Boi fulfill my next order?* I was pretty sure he could, at least I hoped he could.

When I made it to my spot, I gave my out-of-town clientele and told them that my plug would have zones for sale, but he wanted twelve hundred apiece because his last shipment got popped. They told me they were ready to score no matter what the price was.

I'd often heard that the key to success was in the details. So I sat back and thought about details and the practical application of these details in accordance to the big money scheme I was creating.

Chapter 9

After I stashed Teela's Benz, I jumped into my old work truck and headed home. When I pulled into my yard, I heard my neighbors Brenda and Troy arguing. I walked over and asked Brenda what did Troy do this time. She looked at me and said, "His dumbass went partying with his good-for-nothing ass friends and spent all our bill money. Now we can't pay the rent unless we pawn some s——t *once again!*"

Troy sat on the steps of his self-constructed porch with his head in his hands, saying nothing. I told them that I wanted to talk to them in private, so we went inside their home.

The inside was clean but sparsely furnished. The living area sported two mismatched sofas with a small TV, and there was a small table in the kitchen with two chipped old chairs. I sat on one of the sofas, and they took the other one. Brenda looked like she had the brains in the family, so I directed my questions to her.

"Okay," I started, "it seems like you guys are having a hard time. I plan on helping y'all, but I need to know if y'all have jobs already or do you get government assistance to pay bills? And what is the total amount of y'all bills every month?"

Brenda said that they didn't work and relied on disability checks they got, and that their bills ran about $1,200 a month minus food.

I told them that if they wanted, they could work for me and never have to worry about bills ever again.

Brenda asked, "Doing what, Slim?"

"I need you to be my eyes and ears on the streets, watch my house, and follow orders that I will give from time to time," I replied.

"How much does this job pays?" asked Troy.

Brenda yelled, "It doesn't matter because it's all going on bills! Slim, we would love to work for you as long as you keep your word."

I reached into my pocket and gave Brenda $3,000 for her bills. Then I peeled off five more hundreds, gave it to Troy, and told him that was spending money; and if he followed orders, he could expect way more. I asked Brenda who did they rent from.

"The old White man, Mr. Witmore, who lives down the street in that redbrick house on the corner. As a matter of fact, he owns three trailers on this street," she responded.

I gave Brenda a throwaway cell and told her to keep it near her at all times. Then I jumped in my truck and went to see Mr. Witmore.

I pulled up in front of his house and saw him and his wife sitting under a tree, sipping drinks and enjoying the warm summer breeze. *Life must be good for them*, I thought.

He walked up to me and asked, "What can I do for you, son?"

I smiled and said, "I heard that you own three trailer homes on this street, and I wanted to see if I could buy them, along with the lots they're on."

"Well, I wasn't exactly looking to sell, but I suppose for the right price, almost anything can be bought," he said as laughter wheezed out of his mouth.

"So what is the right price?" I asked.

He squinched his eyes together, then said, "If you can come up with thirty thousand, I will let you have everything."

I smiled and said, "If you donate them to me, I will give you fifty thousand cash under the table."

He smiled and said, "You know, the funny thing is that me and the missus was just talking about donations." Wheezing again, he said, "Just give me your information and go get that money for me."

We shook hands, and I went and got his money.

When I came back, I told him to inform the current renters that their new landlord was a Black woman named Mrs. Teela.

Then I called Teela and told her to swing by all the families and let them know that she bought the properties, then for her to try and get them on our payroll.

"You are full of surprises, but all your moves are on point. I will handle that ASAP," she said and hung up.

Next, I called my clientele and told them that I had two hundred zones for sale. They wanted the whole lot, so I went to the country, grabbed the dope, and made three consecutive stops, handling deliveries.

Then I headed back to the country with $240,000. As soon as I sat down, my phone went off; it was Teela.

"Slim, I got two of the families on the payroll, but one family was so mad because I was Black that they started packing their s———t up to move out. They didn't even give me a chance to holler at them," she said.

"Damn, that's crazy! They're letting their racism cause them to miss out on their blessings. F———k 'em! Just have the new members move into it for right now and be at my house eight o'clock tomorrow morning, tastefully dressed for a business meeting."

When we hung up, I turned my phone off, took a shower, then slept the sleep of a dead man. No dreams came, only peaceful blackness.

Chapter 10

I woke up early the next morning fully rejuvenated. After getting myself together, I put $230,000 inside my duffle bag. I met up with a very tastefully dressed Teela, who was sporting a Channel pantsuit and high heels. "Damn! Teela, you look delicious," I remarked.

"If we had time, I would let you get a taste," she responded.

"A rain check is definitely in effect," I said.

She asked, "Where are we going?"

"To see a lawyer because it's time to dot some Is and cross some Ts," I told her.

I had found out about an up-and-coming lawyer who was building a great reputation in the criminal defense world, and I wanted her on the team. Her name was Karen White. We entered the building and, ten minutes later, were shown to a tastefully decorated office. She was tiny in stature, but I noticed that she possessed predatory eyes. I liked that.

We introduced ourselves and sat down.

"So what can I do for you, Mr. Thomas," she asked.

"Well, Teela here and I have a ten-member family of boys who get into trouble from time to time, so I would like to put you on retainer just in case something pops up," I said.

She sat quietly for a moment, then told me that fifty thousand would be required for that many individuals. I nodded, then told her that I had $150,000 more with me and asked if it was possible for her to find us a house in a very remote place that would be big enough to accommodate us all.

She said that she could handle that for us, so I took $200,000 out of the bag and placed it on her desk. I gave Teela the bag with the remaining money. Then I told Mrs. White that I was the head of our household, and Teela was my second-in-command, and that Teela would be the one handling most of the day-to-day business for our family. She told me that she fully understood what I was saying. We did some paperwork, stood up, and shook hands, then Teela and I departed.

When we got in the car, I told Teela to send Mrs. White an email with the names of all our members. I took my phone out and called Brenda.

"Hey! What's up, Slim?" she answered.

"Is there anything happening on your end?" I asked.

"Hell yeah! We got a new landlord who bought us a house full of new furniture, and some new people have moved into that big double-wide trailer down the street, five brothers it looks to be. Oh, our new landlord is a young Black woman by the name of Mrs. Teela who is cool as hell," responded Brenda.

I told Brenda that I was going to be storing some things in the closet of her back room, and it would be delivered to her later on that night, and that her job was to make sure that it went untouched and kept safe, and she would receive five thousand for her troubles. She told me it was all good, then hung up.

I dropped Teela off, then headed to the country to get the zones together: one hundred for Brenda, one hundred for Teela, and 250 for the new members.

I waited until it was dark to bring the load to Teela with instructions. She asked me if her debut was still on track for the next night. I told her it was, and I was on my way to buy something to wear for it. She walked up to me, kissed me, and said, "Slim, I feel like I'm on a rocket, heading straight the f——k up!"

I smiled and said, "Since they lied to us about the forty acres and a mule, we're going to make s——t happen on our own, but, Teela, it takes a lot of careful planning and flawless execution. By the way, send Lil 'G' out to buy another all-black SUV for the other boys."

I kissed her and left.

I bought myself a throwback Houston Oilers jersey, a pair of white Jordan windsuit pants, and some powder-blue-and-white, North Carolina colored Jordan's. It was a nice fit, not too over the top.

After all, I was the self-proclaimed shadow boss. I told Teela to make sure the crew all wore black, but that she was to wear something light colored and sexy so she would stand out. She told me that she had the perfect outfit in mind.

The next day, I sat on my porch, sipping cold beer in the shade. Brenda and Troy joined me. They were all smiles and holding hands. I asked how was life treating them, and they told me fine, thanks to me and their new landlord. Then Brenda said, "We just wanted you to know that your stuff was safe and sound."

"Cool, I will give you instructions on what to do with it as time goes on. Are you guys worried about what y'all are holding for me?" I asked.

Troy smiled and said, "Slim, as good as you treat us, it could be a dead body involved, and we wouldn't trip."

I told him that I would hold them to that, and we all laughed. I thanked them for the good work they were doing for me, then I got up and walked to my crew's trailer.

As I neared the home, I noticed that both SUVs were getting washed by some guy from the neighborhood. Tugga saw me and opened the door for me, saying, "Slim, what's up? Everybody is here."

I stood in the middle of the room and looked at each individual with expressed scrutiny. Then I took a seat in a comfortable big chair after learning the names of the new members, which were Smoke, Cutter, Jaybird, Crump, and Big Mosses.

I began to speak.

Chapter 11

"Anything and everything is possible, and all goals set can be achieved. But it all starts with an idea, and that idea spawns possibility after possibility. Then before you know it, your very reality has been altered.

"And that's what we are doing by creating this squad. For us to be successful, everybody has to play their part. I not only need you all to wear many hats but also to believe in my vision. Believe that if you follow my orders, our reality and the realities of our loved ones will change for the better. S——t is simple from here on out. If you f——k with us, you win, but if you go against us, you lose. Tonight will be a celebration of liberation, so I'm naming our squad the *free money boyz*."

I stood up with my fist raised and yelled, "FMB!"

They all stood up and joined me. Then I gave last-minute instructions for Teela's debut and left.

I headed out to the country to pick up Teela's Benz. Halfway back into town, I called Teela and told her to meet me on the highway so we could exchange cars. I parked at a rest stop and waited for her.

When she pulled up, we both got out and walked toward each other. She smiled and said, "Ooh, I'm glad to have my baby back!"

I laughed and said, "You deserve this and everything else that are coming your way. Listen, Chrisville and Money Mike will want to score big, so if the hundred zones you have stashed ain't enough, send Rambeezy by Brenda's."

I kissed and walked toward her old-school Cutlass, then left to go and get ready.

On my way home, I called Chrisville, and he answered right away, "What it do, Slim? I hope you have some good news for us."

"Yeah, my boy told me that Teela will be at Club Nitrous tonight, and she's agreed to holla at me. Now everybody knows that time is money, so whatever y'all plan on spending, get it together now so I can grab that for y'all ASAP. I suggest that y'all spend as much as y'all can because once she opens up shop, everybody and their mommas will try to score," I responded.

"I feel you on that, so I will holler at Mike and see what he can come up with because I can do one-fifty. I will hit you up in a few," he said, then hung up.

After Teela's debut, I planned on flooding the streets with that hard white. Ten minutes later, Chrisville hit me back and told me to swing by and grab the $300,000 that they had put together. I turned around and headed into the heart of the South side.

When I got there, Chrisville and Money Mike were smiling like in the days of old when they thought that they were still scoring from Big Boi. While me and Mike talked, Chrisville put the bag on my back seat. They told me that they couldn't wait to get it popping again. I told them that if ole girl didn't want to do business, I would give them their money back at the club. We shook hands, and I left. I made a quick trip to deposit the $300,000 in the country, then headed home to get dressed.

When I pulled up to the club a few hours later, it was hard to find a parking spot, but I saw Teela and the boys were parked right in front of the club. All the young hustlers were gawking at Teela's Benz. One of the SUVs was parked in the front of her car, and the other one was parked at the back.

I walked into the club, inhaling the smell of that good people were smoking and looking at all the party goers who were dressed to impress. Chrisville and Money Mike appeared at my side as if by magic.

"What's up, Slim baby? Man, it's going down in this b———tch tonight! Your girl, Teela, is in here already. They got the whole back of the club on lock," said Chrisville.

I looked toward the back of the club and saw the free money boyz popping bottles. "Damn! They look like they got their s——t together. I can tell that they're getting that paper. Oh, here comes my boy Lil 'G'," I replied.

"What's up, Louisiana Slim? Are you ready to have that li'l talk with boss lady Teela?" he asked.

I said that I was, and we walked away as Chrisville and Mike watched. When we got close to Teela, Big Mosses stopped me, patted me down, and took my gun from me. Then he cleared me to go through. I knew that Chrisville and Mike watched as the whole play unfolded, so we exaggerated the introductions between myself and Teela. We shook hands, then sat down to talk business.

"Damn! Teela, you look like a real boss. That's what's up! Say, send Rambeezy to go and grab the one hundred you have stashed, the one hundred from Brenda, and here are my keys. Tell him to put it in my trunk with the one hundred I already have in there. I will go back and chill with my clientele and tell them that it's all good," I told her.

"Wow! You're moving three hundred zones in one whop? That's a nice lick," she responded.

"That's nothing, Teela. Before the week is out, we will get off another thousand."

She looked at me with surprise in her eyes.

I smiled and said, "What? You didn't know we had it like that?"

"F——k no! That's big! If a nigga can't believe in your vision, then he's one blind mutha——cka," she replied. She got close and whispered in my ear, "Tonight, after I bust out of here, I want you to come directly to my house." She pulled back and said, "That's an order."

I smiled again and told her that I would be there. Then I got up, shook her hand, then went over to where Chrisville and Mike were chilling.

They were salivating from the mouth as I walked toward them.

Mike said, "Slim, you are one player ass nigga. Looks like Teela was feeling you, so I guess it's all good, huh?"

"Yeah, y'all boys are lucky because she's even giving y'all a deal at just one rack apiece. Now y'all will be getting three hundred zones altogether," I responded.

They both gave me hugs, then asked when were they going to get their package. I told them that inside the next hour Teela would have their s——t sitting in the trunk of my car, and I would receive a text letting me know it was there.

"Wow! Ole girl is 'bout her biz for real."

"That's even better service than we had with Big Boi. Slim, we owe you big time for this, so if you ever need anything, just holler, real talk," said Chrisville.

I got the text, and we all went to my car and concluded our biz.

Chapter 12

I walked back into the club and took a seat against the wall and sent Teela a text, telling her everything went smoothly. I watched as she texted back, saying that she was ready to take it in. I texted back before she left to buy the bar for the whole club, saying that it was all good.

She looked at me and smiled. Then she walked toward the bar with Tugga and Rambeezy at her side. She placed the order with the owner, Mr. Joe. His eyebrows went up in surprise.

With a huge smile plastered on his face, he grabbed his personal mic and yelled, "Mrs. Teela just bought the bar! Free drinks for the rest of the night for everybody!"

Everyone in the club looked at Teela, then cheered. Rambeezy dropped twenty racks on the bar. Teela smiled and walked out of the club. The FMB all got up and followed her out as everybody stared at the procession. Once they were outside, the boys waited until Teela was in her car, then they all got into the two SUVs, and they pulled off like superstars.

After they were gone, I slipped out of the club and headed toward Teela's house. I called her to tell her that I was on my way and for her to tell the squad to be at the trailer at two o'clock the next day.

By the time I made it to her house, the boys were gone. I knocked on the door, and she answered, wearing just her panties and high heels. She looked absolutely amazing. I closed the door behind me, and I gave her a big hug as I palmed her soft big ass. We kissed deeply and passionately for a few minutes. Then she pulled away and grabbed my hand, leading me into her bedroom.

Once inside, she took her panties off, then she sat at the edge of her bed with her legs spread, revealing a very beautiful, inviting, hairless p——ssy. I smiled and undressed as I walked toward her. I bent down and kissed her, then I gently laid her down and removed her shoes and slid into the bed with her.

Still kissing her, I caressed her body, then I penetrated her hot wetness with a powerful stroke that made her arch her back and gasp for air.

She caught on to my rhythm, and we moved like we were on a dance floor, engaged in some sort of erotic dance.

Time seemed to melt as I went deeper and harder until she screamed in ecstasy. The sounds of her screams caused me to bust inside her smoldering heat, collapsing on top of her.

I rolled over to my side and saw that she still had her eyes closed but was smiling. When she finally opened them, she said, "Damn, Slim, what the f——k just happened?"

I smiled and said, "I think we just got married."

She shook her head yes, and we both started laughing.

When I left, I headed back to the country and got some more zones together, doubling up on everything because it was time to shake and bake. When I was done, I swung back by Teela's house and gave her six hundred zones. I kissed her and told her that I would see her at the meeting the next day. I finally went home and slept.

The next morning, I received pictures of three different homes sent over by my lawyer. She said pick one, then give her a call. All three were nice, but the one that caught my eyes was the big farmhouse in a remote section of the woods with the nice-looking barn.

I called Karen and told her that I wanted the farm. She told me that she would need an extra eight thousand for that one.

I told her that Teela would bring her the rest of the money ASAP. Next, I called Teela and told her to meet me at my house. I gave her the money when she got there plus another twenty-five thousand for herself.

When she had left, I walked over to Brenda and Troy's house and gave them each five thousand. I asked if the next package was stashed.

Brenda said, "Yeah, we got it, and it's in good hands. Today is a great day for us because we're buying ourselves a new car."

"Whoa, nah! Y'all are coming up in the world, huh? That's good because as long as y'all are good, I'm good," I responded.

I gave Brenda a key to my house and told her to hold it down just in case I needed her to go inside and handle some biz for me. Then I went home and chilled for a couple of hours. I made some calls to my clientele and told them that from this point on, I would be sending some guys from my crew to handle transactions.

Word spread, and I had sales for 450 more zones. I went back to the country to get it, then I headed to the trailer to meet the crew. Teela called me and told me that all the biz was handled, and that she was on her way to the meeting place. We arrived ten minutes apart, with me being last.

When I walked into the house, everybody yelled, "What's up, boss man?"

I sat down and asked them how did it feel to finally be on top. They told me that last night was unbelievable. I told them that it would only get better. I gave Teela the names and numbers of my out-of-town clientele and told her to send some of the boys to handle the transactions.

"Do you want me to serve them from the stash that you gave me last?" she asked.

"No! I got it all in my trunk. Send Tugga outside to grab it," I replied.

"Damn, Slim! You're not playing any games, huh? You be getting it out the mud for real," she remarked.

I smiled and said, "Boys, pack up because after y'all go and make them drops, we're all heading to our new house."

"What new house, Slim?" asked Lil "G".

I looked his way and said, "I just bought us a big farm out in the country."

They all started cheering. Tugga came back with the bag of dope, and I watched as Teela delegated the drops.

After they were given directions to the farm, I headed out there to wait on them.

The farm was beautiful and well kept. I liked the white brick and the huge wraparound porch. The big pecan trees were awesome, and the barn was just the right size to set up shop for cooking up product because it was far from the house. I was definitely going to get some animals just for show. I went inside, took a look around, and approved of how spacious and clean it was. I walked over to a window, peered outside, and smiled.

Chapter 13

After a couple of hours contemplating my next move and enjoying the fresh country air, I looked up to see Teela and the crew coming down the road that led to our farm.

Everybody parked, got down, and gawked at the big farmhouse in admiration.

Big Mosses said, "So what is this home?"

"More like headquarters?" I responded as everybody gathered on the huge porch.

"Would Unc, I'm feeling this because nobody will be in our business way out here," said Ram.

"There are eight rooms and four bathrooms, and I will be converting that barn into a cooking unit where three of y'all will be working until I can hire some trustworthy people for the job," I told them.

Teela looked my way and said, "Slim, the boys did the runs, plus they also got rid of what I gave them the other day. So I have $700,000 in the trunk."

I looked at everyone and said, "I'm proud of the way y'all are getting s——t done and following orders. Remember, money made is for our family and to help a few unfortunate people that's struggling out there, so never let the idea of stealing from the family enter your mind because if you do, I will consider you our enemy. I promise you it's better to be a part of this family than it's enemy."

I ordered Teela to take $100,000 to get the house laced up and to contact someone to outfit the barn. She was to give everyone present ten grand apiece and replenish the zones that they had sold from the stash I gave her. I told the family to put their stuff in the house, and that I would be back after I stashed the half a mill.

I loaded up the money and went to the country to stash it. I took out 150 racks, then went to see Johnny the Jeweler. When I got there, I told him that I wanted ten pieces and chains with the letters *FMB* in diamonds. He told me that I could pick them up in three days if I added another fifty. I smiled and said, "I respect the hustle, Johnny, so I will have the money for you when I pick everything up."

We shook hands, then I left.

Next, I went to a tech place who specializes in home security and made arrangements to have all footage directed to our headquarters.

When I decided to head back to the farm, I was armed with a kilo of soft white and a couple of microwaves. It was time to give them knowledge about cooking.

It was night when I finally got there; the lonely, beautiful old farmhouse was lit up. When I walked in, everybody was all smiles. The house was already sparsely furnished, so I took a seat, then ordered Smoke to go and grab the microwaves and duffle bag containing the kilo.

When he returned, we all went to the kitchen, and I began giving them all cooking lessons using my money-making formula. They were all shocked by how much extra profit was realized using it. Teela smiled and said, "So that's how you came up so fast, huh?"

"Yeah, that and a lot of luck, nuts, and determination, and instead of being greedy, I decided to put this family together and help put some real niggas on their feet," I responded.

"And make a bad b———tch a boss!" Teela laughed and remarked.

"Yeah! And that too," I said, and everybody laughed.

After the lessons were given, I assigned Smoke, Cutter, and Tugga to cooking detail because their zones came out looking the best.

Then we all gathered in the living room. I looked at them and said, "The only way we will survive this game is if we move as a complete unit and watch one another's back. We have to be willing to bust our guns for one another without hesitation if it comes to that. There's a lot of open land out here if you need to work on your shooting skills. Next week, I will be buyin' more artillery from Adam. Teela, walk me outside because I'm about to bust out."

We walked to my car and sat on the hood, and I brought her up to speed on the security plans and my trip to the jeweler. She grabbed my hand and said, "Baby, you think of everything, and I'm really feeling you. I respect and believe in your vision. Anyway, you better get out of here before I put you in a compromising position." Then she laughed her musical-sounding laughter.

I kissed her in the darkness and said, "I can think of worst things happening to me." Then I got into my car and left.

After Teela got the farm in order, I brought the rest of the kilos out there and gave them to her so she could get the boys to cook them up and package everything.

Johnny called me and said my purchase was ready. I brought him the rest of the money and got the chains. Johnny had outdone himself. I was very pleased with his work. I told him to do another one with L. S. sitting on top of a lion's face. I called Teela and told her to swing by my house in town to get the chains.

I was sitting on my porch, talking to Brenda and Troy, when she pulled up.

Brenda smiled and said, "What's up, landlord?"

Teela smirked, then said, "Slim, let the poor girl know who her real landlord is."

Brenda looked at me with confusion on her face and said, "Slim! What's she talking about?"

I smiled and said, "Brenda, I'm the one who bought the trailer from Witmore."

Brenda and Troy started laughing.

"Then who is Mrs. Teela to you?" she asked.

"Family!" I responded as Teela and I excused ourselves and went into my house.

We started kissing and undressing as soon as I closed the door. After we appeased our hunger, I walked to my room and got the chains while she went into the bathroom to clean up.

When she returned, I gave her the chains. She put hers around her neck and said, "Hell yeah! This makes everything look more official. I love it." She told me that she would pass them out to the boys after she left. We kissed again, then she walked outside and jumped in her Benz and left.

As the weeks went by, we got rid of 90 percent of our inventory. With over three million plus in hard cold cash, it was time to go see Big Boi.

I made a call to Karen and told her I needed her to find me some cattle sellers out of Houston.

Chapter 14

After Karen lined me up with the livestock people, I bought a couple of huge trailers and two big dually trucks to pull them. I got all the boys to dress up like cowhands, and we left for Houston, toting two million plus in cash. Teela brought extra clothes for our meet with Big Boi.

When we arrived in cowboy state, we rented the whole bottom floor of a mildly expensive hotel so the boys could get some rest for the work that had to be done.

I called Big Boi while Teela got dressed; when he answered, he yelled, "Oh, s———t! It's Louisiana Slim! What's been going on with you, my nigga? It's been a long time since you hollered."

I told him that I was in town, and I wanted to talk business and if he would meet me at the Italian place on Roth Street.

"Damn, Slim, why don't you just come by the house like you always do?" he asked.

"I have my girl with me, so it's best we do it this way this time. S———t, you might not want her to know where you lay your head. Hell, she doesn't even know where my real house is yet," I laughed.

"That's why I got big love for you, Slim, because you're always on your s———t. I can meet you in thirty minutes," he hit back, then hung up.

We took Teela's car, and I drove. We enjoyed the warm sun as we carted through the downtown area. When I pulled in, I noticed that Big Boi was already seated inside, next to a huge glass window, looking outside. I saw the surprised expression on his face when Teela and I pulled up and got out of the Benz.

We entered the restaurant and walked toward his table.

He stood up, gave me a hug, and said, "I see you, my nigga! Life is treating you good, huh?"

"I can't complain. This is my girl, Teela, my second-in-command," I responded.

Big Boi smiled and said, "Slim, you say that she's your second-in-command like you have an army or something." Then he laughed.

"Yeah, I have a few loyal soldiers on my team now. Teela here is in charge of day-to-day operations, and she does a great job," was my response.

He looked at me seriously and asked, "How much are you trying to spend?"

I took a sip of my drink, looked him square in the eyes, and said, "Two million."

Air escaped his lungs as a whistling sound came from his lips. "Damn, my nigga! I knew that you were probably hustling hard, but s———t, that's a serious order. I will have to call my plug to fill it. Could you chill for a day at the least while I handle my biz?" he asked.

I told him that wouldn't be a problem because I actually had some other biz to handle as well. With that, we stood up, shook hands, and he told me to expect a call.

Teela and I went back to the hotel, and I called the livestock people and made some arrangements to buy some cattle and a couple of horses for the farm. We were to be there the next morning.

Big Boi called me a few hours later and said, "Slim, I made that call to my plug Mr. M, and he wants to set up a meet with you and your crew before he sells you the dope. So tomorrow we will all go to one of his homes that he has down here at three o'clock."

I told him that we would swing by his spot if it was all right with him, then follow him to his plug's home. He told me that it was all good, and that I should meet him at about two thirty.

After I got off the phone with Big Boi, I explained everything that was going down with Teela. I instructed her to have the boys on high alert and fully armed when we would go to the meet. She assured me that they would be, and we hung up and got some rest.

Six o'clock the next morning, the crew and I headed out to get the cattle and the horses. The place was huge and well stocked with all manner of farm animals. Mr. Jake, who owned the operation, asked, "Mr. Thomas, would you be willing to buy five and five? Because if you are, I will throw in free feed and saddles for the horses."

"Sounds like a good deal. Just have your guys direct my guys with the loading of the animals. I trust you to pick out the best because I'm sure we will be doing more business in the future. Mrs. Teela will pay the bill," I told him.

We shook hands, and I took a look around, admiring the huge variety of animals that they had.

At two o'clock, the crew and I headed out to Big Boi's house, all of us dressed in black. We went in a couple of SUVs that I rented for the little excursion. I ordered Cutter to stay at the hotel and guard the animals.

When we neared Big Boi's house, I called him and told him that we were turning on his street. He was walking out of his doorway with two of his guys when we drove up. Big Boi looked around and said, "Damn! You wasn't bull——ting when you told me you had a few soldiers, huh?"

I smiled and said, "S——t, a nigga can never be too careful, especially moving around with two million in cash."

"Yeah, I feel you on that. Well Mr. M is waiting, so y'all just follow me," he said as he got in the back seat of his Lexus.

He took us through the downtown area, then we headed out. We ended up in a beautiful gated community. The homes were all beautiful, and it was like I could smell the money in the air.

The home that we went to looked like a baby mansion. When we were let into the gates, we rounded the curved driveway and parked. I saw that this Mr. M also had a private little army. They were strategically positioned around his estate. I was very impressed.

We all got down and were greeted by one of his minions. He led us into a little maze that ended with us standing in the biggest backyard I ever saw. A group of men were studying us in silence as we approached.

Three of them looked like muscle, one looked like he knew things of high value, but the Armani-clad Mexican-looking gentleman in the middle had to be Mr. M.

Chapter 15

My guys stopped at a safe distance as the rest of us walked up to the awaiting men. Mr. M smiled, exposing even pearly white teeth and said, "Aah, I'm happy that you all made it safely."

Big Boi made the introductions, then we all sat down to discuss business. Mr. M, whose real name was Martinez, looked at me and asked, "If I decide to sell you the kilos, how will you transport it safely across the state line?"

"Well that's really the easy part because I was down here buying cattle and horses for my farm, which we already have loaded up and ready to go. So after we leave here, my guys will transform into cowhands, and the kilos will be placed among the animals. I think they will provide a nice disguise for what I'm really moving," I responded.

"I like the idea because you always want to be as careful as you can, especially whenever you're just starting to get your feet wet. Two million is a very nice purchase for a guy who started from nothing. It clearly shows that you have the drive, the brain, and the ability to move a lot of coke. So here is what I propose. You want 180 kilos for the two million, but I will give you four hundred instead to take with you to sell at your own pace. All I want is 2.5 million for the extra 220 that I'll give to you on consignment. But I want you to know something. If you agree, we will do business for a long time, but you need to know that I'm not a man that you would want to play games with," said Martinez.

I looked at him unblinkingly and said, "Mr. Martinez, I appreciate the offer, but I will have to decline. I only want what I came to buy and nothing else. But I can assure you that every time I need to score, it will be with you, and I will most definitely keep our business confidential. Now if you want to give me extra kilos as part of the two million deal that we are making, then I will accept, which I think is somewhat in your best interest to do because the more product I have to sell, the more money you can expect me to spend on my next trip."

Martinez was silent for a few seconds, then said, "So you want extra kilos without the responsibility of consignment. It's very smart of you to point out that it would be in my best interest to build up your inventory since I will be your sole provider. Tough negotiator you are, Mr. Thomas, but very astute. So here is what I will do. For the money you have, I will let you leave here with 250 kilos."

I signaled for Mosses to bring the bag of money for Mr. Martinez, and while we sat back and had drinks, his people went and got the product for my people. Martinez gave me his private number and wished me luck.

I thanked Big Boi for hooking me up with his plug and told him that if he ever needed me, I would come through for him.

We loaded up the kilos and left for the hotel where we changed back into our farming clothes. After returning the rentals, we hit the highway.

When we made it back to our farm safely, the boys unloaded the animals. Teela and I went to my private room to talk. She closed the door and gave me a hungry kiss. Then she pulled back and said, "I've been wanting to do that all day!" Then she laughed.

"Yeah, I feel you on that because this trip was super intense, but I think it's safe to say we are about to control the North and South side of this region. I'm leaving you fifty kilos to get cooked and packaged, so hire some more trustworthy cookers. Also I want you to call Karen tomorrow and let her know that you will be dropping by to bring her fifty thousand, and that I appreciated her help in finding the livestock people," I told her. I gave her another kiss as I placed my hand between her legs and squeezed.

She moaned and said, "Don't start nothing that you can't finish."

I smiled, then walked out the door.

After we got everything up and rolling, the money started pouring in at an unbelievable rate. I had to invest in more counting machines along with a huge safe.

I decided to call Martinez to discuss a little problem that I was having. He answered promptly, asking, "Slim, how are you doing? Don't tell me that you're ready for another trip already, huh?"

I laughed and said, "No, but I'm having a problem with all the money that's stacking up on my end. I need a way to get it cleaned, but I don't have the resources. I was hoping you could help me out. I really need to get stabilized before I make my return trip your way next month."

"Okay, I understand, and I think I can help you with that. As a matter of fact, I know a guy in your neck of the woods who I can call to set up a meet with you," he responded.

The next day, Teela and I entered the Trust One Bank on Commerce Street. We were met by a bookish-looking White guy wearing an expensive suit who went by the name Mr. Wilbrooks. He ushered us into his private office.

"So, Mr. Thomas, I hear that you need to get some dirt off your hands. Well I can assist you with that at a 10 percent charge on every million, assuming you are trying to get such amount cleaned at one time. Your money will be taken care of by us and become legitimized and able to be spent anyway that you wish. Now how much do you want to get cleaned at the moment?" he asked.

I sat back and thought of everything that he said and told him that I wanted four million cleaned and ready to be used as soon as possible. I told him that Teela was to have access to 50 percent of the funds because she would be handling the bulk of the business.

He told me that would be fine, and he would start the paperwork as soon as I brought the money in. I told him that I had the money outside in the trunk of my car.

"Wow! You waste no time. I like that. Well bring it in directly, and we can start the process."

After a couple of hours, we walked out of the bank and into the bright sunshine; we headed out to our favorite Mexican restaurant to talk business.

When we were seated, Teela said, "Slim, I cannot believe how fast we've come up in the game. Just imagine what we can do with legit money at our disposal."

"Yeah, I came up with the idea because stability is the key now. It's FMB for life now, baby, so there will be no walking away from here on out," I countered.

Chapter 16

As Teela and I talked, a thought occurred to me. I said, "Teela, we run this North side. Chrisville and Money Mike got the South on lock with me as their plug, but only a small fraction of our product is trickling down at fluctuating prices on the East and West sides. So I think I will put some feelers out there and find out who's supplying them, then undercut their prices. So whenever I get the info, I will set up a meet with us and them. We need to control this whole region."

"Yeah, I think that's a great idea because that way you will be able to control all the beef and dumb s——t that'll be popping off," she replied.

"That's my thinking exactly, plus we will be able to move more kilos at an even faster rate. So get the boys together for a trip to the West and East sides. I want you to fill two duffle bags with five hundred zones apiece."

When I got the intel I needed, FMB rolled out to the West side to holler a cat by the name of Tiny Tim who was running s——t. We met up at a little gambling operation that he had. We were geared up in black, wearing our chains.

I came out of the shadows for this meet, sporting the L. S. ion chain. We were all strapped. When we rolled up, all eyes were on us. We walked into the establishment as a unit and was met by Tiny Tim. We shook hands, then he led us into a side room for some privacy.

I looked at Tim and said, "As you know, they call me Louisiana Slim or just Slim for short. Here is the deal, I'm in position to help you get rich, but to do this, I need to know who's supplying you and how much they're charging for their product."

"Well I get them at $1,500 a zone from a couple of cats on the South side named Chrisville and Money Mike."

Teela looked at me and started laughing. Tiny Tim looked at her with confusion in his eyes and asked, "Why is that so funny?"

"Because we're the ones supplying them at a lower price, and since they've been f——cking over y'all, I'm going to sell you two hundred zones for a rack a piece. Then front you another three hundred more for $500 apiece. That way, you will be able to build up your inventory and your capital, and the faster you move them, the more I will front you. The number has no limit., Aas long as you do good business and stay loyal to FMB, you will never run out of product."

Tim looked at me with his mouth hanging and shock plastered on his face as he finally yelled, "Goddamn it! I had a feeling that today was going to be a good day. Slim, if you're coming like that, I'm in, and I can promise you that the West side will be a 100 percent loyal to you."

I told Cutter to go and get the package, and Tiny Tim sent for the $200,000 to complete the deal. Before we left, I told Tim that if any kind of beef kicked off, I wanted to be notified immediately because getting money was now everybody's top priority.

Business concluded, we exchanged numbers, and I let Tim know that Teela was my second-in-command, running the day-to-day operations.

"So that means that I will be dealing with her mostly then?" he asked.

"Yeah! That's correct, and never let anyone disrespect her in any way, is that understood?" I asked.

He nodded his head up and down.

After the meet with Tiny Tim, we ventured to the East side to meet up with this guy called Cambright at an old warehouse that he owned. I secured the same deal with him.

After the huge success and $400,000 richer, we headed back to the farm. Once we got in the house, we got some drinks and sat down to discuss some things.

"Listen up, fam. As we continue to spread out like we're doing, money will be coming in faster than it is now, so that means transporting is vital upon rescoring. Therefore, I'm going to try and buy us a moving company. That way, we can hit the highway unnoticed. I'm sure it won't be a problem, so be ready to wear that hat on the next trip, okay?

"Well I'm going to go upstairs and get some rest because tomorrow I will have to do some more shaking and baking. Teela, come with me for a minute," I said.

Rambeezy looked at Big Mosses, laughed, and said, "Slim, you and Teela may as well get married!"

Teela looked at them, smirked, then said, "Lil nigga, you're late. Me and Slim have been married for a couple of months now."

Everybody started cheering.

Cutter said, "Well I wish y'all the best because you two are the best bosses that a nigga could ever have."

Teela stopped in her tracks and said, "Speaking on that side of business, tomorrow I'm going to get Wilbrooks to open up accounts in each one of your names, starting at fifty thousand apiece because you b——tches are my sons!"

Everyone cheered and laughed.

When Teela and I were alone, she kissed me, then said, "Slim, I hope I didn't f——k up telling the boys about us."

"Nah, it's all good. They're not crazy and have probably known about us from the start because you're too beautiful and fine to just be single, and if one of them wasn't hitting the p——ssy, that means I probably was."

"Also they never see me f——cking with other women, so they knew," I assured her as I took her clothes off.

We fell into the bed and became one. She gave herself over to me like she had never done before. We explored and connected on many levels that night.

When we were both sated, she lay on my chest and said, "It feels good to have this part of our relationship out in the open."

"Yeah, because now I don't have to worry about anyone approaching you, thinking that they could get some of that good you have. Plus, it will add more weight to your name," I told her.

She agreed, and we drifted off to sleep.

The next day, I was on the phone, discussing a list of foreclosed properties that his bank had for sale and for him to be on the lookout for a moving company preferably small that was for sale.

A couple of hours later, I was in his office, spending 1.2 million on a bunch of foreclosed properties and a small moving company that wasn't getting much business.

Our new company had a nice warehouse and three moving trucks. The forty homes I got for pennies on a dollar would become great assets that could be used as, for example, various stash spots for a few of them. The FMB empire was growing.

Chapter 17

"Chrisville, I think I got a good lick for us, bro," said Money Mike.

"What the f——k are you talking about, nigga?" asked Chrisville.

"I got word from a smoker who says that that b——tch Teela is stashing dope inside that trailer next door to that nigga Slim's house, and it's supposed to be major weight. The smoker said there is just one White girl and her ole man guarding it. I say we hit that spot tonight along with a couple of other niggas and get some of that free money they be bragging about," said Money Mike.

"S——t, man, I don't know if we should f——k with that. Besides, she's our plug," responded Chrisville.

"Man, we're gonna be masked up and s——t, so they won't know who did it. Just to make sure, we can ask that nigga Slim if he thinks the stash spot is legit," said Mike as he placed the call.

*****

I was with the squad when I got the call from Mike.

"Oh, what's up, Mike?" I asked.

"Listen, Slim, me and Chrisville are trying to hit a lick tonight if it's good, but we want to make sure before we run up in that b——tch. We heard ole girl Teela is stashing dope at that trailer next to your house. Have you ever seen her go and drop s——t off over there?" asked Money Mike.

I was shocked to hear him ask me that. I knew he was a slimeball but not on this sort of level.

"What do I get out of the deal if I give you some information?" I asked.

"S——t, man, you know we're going to break you off!" he said.

"Well I have seen her go there and drop some s——t off. As a matter of fact, late last night I saw her and one of them FMB niggas carry two duffle bags in there. They didn't know that I peeped in my window and watched them," I told him as everyone in the house listened to my conversation in angry silence.

"Okay, Slim, thanks. After we hit them b——tches, we will break you off a little something," he said and hung up.

I looked at Teela and said, "Them b——tch a——s niggas Chrisville and Money Mike found out about one of our stash spots and plan on running in it tonight and rob the place."

"*What*! I knew they were some f——k boys the first time I laid my eyes on them! What do you want us to do? Because I already know that you have a plan of action for us to follow," she asked.

"Yeah, I want you to call Brenda and Troy and tell them to stay at my house tonight and not to come outside until tomorrow. Then place three hundred zones inside the trailer in a spot that can be easily found so their little robbery can go fast and smooth.

"After they the lick, I want them followed so we can find out where they stash their s——t. So that means we need someone chilling inside a car on every consecutive street from ours. That way, all directions will be covered. We've made this rise to top, and nobody is going to f——k with us in a bad way and live to tell the tale."

I stood up and yelled, "FMB!"

The squad stood up and yelled, "For life!"

I called Tiny Tim and told him that I had some murda business that I wanted him to handle. I asked him if he was down to bust his gun for me.

"F——cking A, Slim. Just point the nigga out, and I'ma dome check his b——tch a——s, leave him brainless, know what I'm saying?" he asked.

"Cool, I will swing by and pick you up later, my nigga," I remarked.

Later on that night, we were strategically positioned, waiting on the arrival of the jack boys. While Tim and I were chilling in a car on the next street over, I got a call from Cutter, telling me that they saw four niggas creeping toward the trailer.

*****

"Chrisville, go ahead and kick the door in, and we will come in right behind you," whispered Money Mike.

Chrisville did as he was told, and they all entered as soon as the door swung open. They were surprised to find the house empty.

"Close the door, nigga!" Chrisville whispered to one of the guys who was with them.

After the door was closed, they began their search for the dope. A few minutes later, Money Mike said, "Yo! I think I got it!"

They all gathered into the back room as

Money Mike unzipped one of the duffel bags, finding it filled with what looked like one hundred zones.

Chrisville whispered, "BINGO! That dumb bitch got all this issue just laying in here. Let's grab this shit and get the fuck outta here before someone comes home."

FMB followed at a safe distance to the little street that led to the highway. The jack boys had grabbed the bags, crept out, then quickly ran onto the next street where their getaway black van sat waiting for them. Now turning off the highway, they drove slowly and confidently toward their hideout in the secluded wooded area.

I ordered the squad to not turn and follow them but to keep straight for a couple of minutes.

Dressed in all black, we exited our vehicles and went the rest of the way on foot. Fifteen minutes later, we came upon a solitary wooden house, where the black van was parked. I peeped inside one of the windows and saw the four of them sitting together, counting their booty. I gave the signal, and we crashed through the front and back doors simultaneously.

The men inside gave startled yelps and tried to go for their guns, but Rambeezy shot one of them directly in the head, spraying blood and bone fragments everywhere as the guy's head exploded. The rest of them immediately raised their hands in surrender. We were all masked up, so they hadn't seen our faces yet, but I assumed they knew who we were because the unknown guy with them screamed, "Man, they paid me to go into that house with them!"

Chrisville looked around at all the guns pointed at him and pleaded for his life. We all started removing our masks. Fear turned into terror as recognition sat in.

Money Mike screamed, "Slim! You set us up, you dirty mutha———cka!"

Teela walked up to him and slapped him violently across his face and said, "Don't talk to our boss like that!"

Money Mike's eyes widened as he stammered, "Ba-Ba-Ba-Boss?"

I laughed and said, "Yeah, this is my crew, you dumbass niggas. I'm the head of FMB. Now here is the deal. Only one of you is leaving here alive tonight, and it all depends on my nigga Tim." I turned toward Tim and said, "Eeny, meeny, miny, moe, one of these b———tch ass niggas."

Tim walked up to Money Mike and blew his brains out. The sound of the 9 mm was deafening. Chrisville screamed.

Chapter 18

With anger in my eyes, I looked a Chrisville and told him to *shut the f——k up*! Then I told him I wanted to know where all there hustling money was. He said that they kept it in a safe in the back room. I sent a couple of the boys to escort him and retrieve the money.

They came back moments later, carrying two duffle bags and placed them at my feet. I peeped inside of the bags and said, "Damn! Ya lil niggas been hustling real good. Now I don't even understand why y'all wanted to f——k with Teela when all y'all had to do was bring her all this money to score. Then instead of stealing from her, she would have given you the same amount that you stole for free. But I guess haters just hate for the f——k of it. We appreciate this li'l donation that you just gave us though, good looking out," I said as I walked outside hand in hand with Teela.

As we walked away, we heard the blast of a shotgun and watched as FMB emerged, holding all the bags. Tugga and Big Mosses set the house ablaze. The orange fire cast an eerie light against the blackness of the night. We made it to our cars and peeled off into the night.

The family headed to the farm, and I headed toward the West side to drop Tiny Tim off. We rode back in silence as I thought about the night's events. When we got there, I told him that the no hesitation on his part was a real act of true loyalty, and that I appreciated it.

"No doubt, boss!" he said as he got out of the car and disappeared into the darkness among his gambling houses.

When I finally made it back to the farm, Teela already had the money counted and stashed. She looked my way and said, "Can you believe that them hoe ass niggas had 1.7 million stashed and was still trying to hit a dirty lick?"

"The dirty lick threw me for a loop, but the amount they had stashed didn't. I want you to add $100,000 apiece to everyone's account and send Tiny Tim his share tomorrow," I responded as I went upstairs and took a shower.

The next day, I called a meeting, and we all sat under one of the big pecan trees.

"I just wanted to say that I like the way y'all handled biz last night, especially you, Rambeezy, so I'm promoting you. As of now, you will take over the South side. Take four soldiers with you along with two thousand zones and flood that b———tch for the low a $450 a zone.

"Teela, get with Wilbrooks and see if you can get a nice house in the South so Rambeezy can open up shop. The game is wicked and can go from zero to a hundred in no time at all. That's why we have to stay on our toes. Trust no one but family," I told them.

I called Brenda.

"What's up, Slim?" she asked.

"Listen, I want y'all to go and take your personal belongings out of the trailer, then move into my house. I will send some of my people to get my personal stuff out of my house. Everything in the house belongs to you now, including the house, but the trailer is still your responsibility to watch over, so keep it up, okay?" I asked.

"You know we got you, Slim, and thanks for everything," she said, then hung up.

"Teela, let's take a ride to the car lot. It's time for me to buy something for myself to roll in," I said.

"It's about time because I'm tired of seeing you roll in that old boy Caprice," she said and laughed.

*****

"So what are you interested in, Mr. Thomas?" asked the car salesman.

I told him that I wanted two Bentley trucks, one all black with red guts, and the other white with blue guts. I wanted the rims matching the interior. "Teela, translate to him what I want while I have a talk with the owner," I remarked.

Leaving them, I entered the office of Mr. Coffers. We shook hands, then I took a seat. I asked him if he could give me a deal on ten modest family-oriented Benzes plus the two Bentley trucks that I had the salesman working on.

"I'm trying to pay in the range of $50,000 apiece for the cars and a little less than the standard price for the trucks. I would like all the vehicles to be delivered to this address," I said as I slid a piece of paper to him.

"Wow! That's a very large purchase, but it won't be a problem. How will you be paying, Mr. Thomas?" he asked.

I smiled, then said in full from my personal account from Trust One Bank on Commerce.

He jumped up and took me to see the cars. After I selected the vehicles and finalized the paperwork, Teela and I left.

"Why was the owner showing you cars, baby?" she asked.

"Because I bought a few of them. I want you to pick out ten of the best houses that we have and put the keys and photos of houses and properties in ten separate envelopes. Then put a name of each member of the squad on them. Then I want you to set up a cook out here at the farm and tell the crew to invite their moms so I can talk to them," I instructed.

"Done! Oh, I just wanted you to know that we have eight million in dirt. What do you want me to do with it?" she asked.

"Take three million to Wilbrooks and get the rest of it outfitted into the moving trucks for the trip to Martinez this weekend. Since he gave me 250 kilos for two mil, I'm thinking that I can get him to give me six hundred for five mil. Once we get six hundred kilos, there will be no looking back. We're going to shoot straight into the stratosphere where the weather is great!" I replied.

She smiled, leaned over, and kissed me, then said, "You da man, homie!"

The next morning, the vehicles arrived, and I had them park the cars in the backyard. We then placed a set of keys inside each one of the envelopes.

Teela had some guys from the hood cooking while the sound system jammed some Isley Brothers. The tables were set up in front of the house.

After everyone arrived, I called for a meeting inside the house for the squad and their moms. They all sat in silence as I began talking, "I want to thank everybody for coming. Ladies, I'm sure you want to know why your sons invited you out to this farm. Well they probably didn't tell you, but they own this farm." I saw the looks of surprise on the mom's faces as I revealed that bit of news. "You see, we created this extended family so we could survive in the streets and provide for our loved ones, and nobody loves anyone more than they love mom's duce."

Chapter 19

"With that in mind, we've taken the liberty of getting you beautiful ladies some things to show how much you're appreciated. Teela, please pass out the envelopes." As the women looked inside the big envelopes, we heard loud gasps escaped their lips. "Inside are the keys to your own homes, and you each now have a new car, which is parked in the backyard, so please follow me so y'all can check out your new rides." The women cheered, then hugged and thanked their sons. They were overcome with joy as tears streamed down their faces.

After everybody regained control of themselves, I yelled, "Now let's party!"

We danced, laughed, and enjoyed one another's company. Before the party broke up, I made the necessary arrangements to have the homes deeded to each new owner. The crew gave me thanks for pulling the surprise off for their mothers.

Tugga said, "Man, my momma never hugged me like that before! Now I would like that ole nigga she's with try and say something bad about me."

We all started laughing.

I got their attention and said, "All right, fellas, I want everybody ready Friday morning for a trip to Martinez's house so we can get our inventory straight."

I sent Teela on an errand, and while she was gone, I told the boys that we were going to make another big purchase.

"What kind of purchase?" asked Cutter.

"I want to buy Club Nitrous and rename it Club Teela," I smiled and told them.

"Hell yeah! That would be awesome, and for all the work she does, she most definitely deserves it," said Big Mosses.

I looked at everyone and said, "We will surprise her with it after the trip with a huge opening of free drinks all night. I'll try and get the Northside Head Busters to perform. I want it to be lit!"

Lil "G" smiled and said, "Man, I love this family." Then he yelled, "FMB for life!"

We all raised our fists and yelled the same in unison.

The next day, I went and talked to Mr. Joe, the owner of Club Nitrous, about buying the place from him. I found him inside his office. When he saw me, he smiled and said, "Louisiana Slim! What brings you by at this time of the day?"

I shook his hand, took a seat, and said, "Business."

He looked at me with uncertainty in his huge brown eyes and asked, "What kind of business are you referring to?"

"Well I'm interested in taking this club off your hands. I know that you've put a lot of time and energy into this place, but at your age, you must be thinking about retirement," I remarked.

As he looked at me with newfound interest, he laughed, stopped writing, then leaned back with his fingers laced behind his head and said, "Hell! Everybody dreams of retiring, but you see, in my case, I'm up to my ears in debt. Over $100,000 to be exact because somewhere along the way, I made some bad decisions. So if you can appreciate my situation, then you can understand why I wouldn't be able to sell out. If I did, I wouldn't get enough profit for retirement. I'm trapped by my big dream of becoming a club owner."

"How much do you think your club is worth minus the debt?" I asked.

"Well given the location and how well kept this building is, I would think at least $150,000, stock included," he countered.

I smiled and said, "Well today is your lucky day because I really want this club as a surprise for a lady friend of mine. So here is what I'm willing to do for you. Before I buy it right out, I'm going to pay all your outstanding debts, then I'm going to give you $300,000 for this place plus another $100,000 if you continue to run it for her for at least a month so she can have a smooth transition into becoming an owner."

He looked at me with his big eye bulging out of its sockets and said, "My god, man! Are you serious? Because if you are, then you've got yourself a deal!"

I took out my cell and called Mr. Wilbrooks and told him about the deal I had just made, and that we were on the way to his office to get the ball rolling. He told me that he would be expecting us.

I looked at Mr. Joe and said, "Let's take a ride over to Trust One Bank and do some business."

When we got outside and slid into my black Benz truck, Mr. Joe said, "Now this is a nice truck. I didn't know you had it like that!"

I smiled and said, "As a matter of fact, I have a matching white one with the baby blue interior, and when we get to the bank, you will see that I've been on my money s———t."

When we got to the bank, we went into Mr. Wilbrooks's office, and he stood up, then said, "Mr. Thomas, I appreciate all the recent business that you've been giving us. We want you to know that you are a very valued client. So you want to buy this club and wipe this gentleman's slate clean? Seems like you're creating a lovely portfolio for yourself. I don't see any problems with your request. Are there any more specifics that I need to be aware of?" he asked.

"Yeah, I want Teela to be the sole owner of this club, so I'll have her come in next week and sign all the proper papers. I'm buying it as a surprise gift for all the hard work she's done," I told him.

"Well consider it taken care of," he replied.

I got up, looked at Mr. Joe, and told him that I would be waiting across the street at the new burger place while he took care of business.

About an hour later, he found me sitting in my truck as he walked out of the bank looking years younger. He jumped in the truck and said, "Man! I can't believe it. I don't owe nobody s———t! Son, I don't know how to thank you."

I nodded and said, "It's all good. Now here is what I need you to do. I want the Club Nitrous sign replaced with Club Teela, and I want a place set up against the center wall as her personal space with the words *Northside Queen* with a throne underneath it. Spare no expense because I want it all done for Saturday's grand opening. Just give me the finished bill. Oh, the drinks will be free all night, so I want us to be fully stocked. Any questions?" I asked.

"No, I got it, boss," he replied.

Before we left for the trip, I had secured the rap group at the cost of $30,000.

Friday morning, we were all on the road headed to Martinez's place. With five million on hand, we would make a purchase that would solidify us as the head niggas in charge. Teela looked at me, smiled, and crossed her fingers.

Chapter 20

When our squad turned on the road heading toward Martinez's estate, I called him.

"What's going on, Slim?" he asked.

"Well I'm down the street from your house with my family. I hope it's a good time for a visit," I told him.

"It's a great time for a visit. My door is always open to you. I'll have my people let you in," he responded.

When we got inside the gates, we parked and got out of our vehicles. This time, we were led into the house.

"Damn! Mr. Martinez, this place looks like a palace," I said as I looked around in awe.

He smiled his beautiful smile and said, "At the rate you're going, I have no doubt that you will be enjoying the same comforts as I am. So I take it that you want to replenish your inventory. What are you spending this time?" he asked as he pointed for me to sit in the cream leather chair next to his.

"Well I'm trying to see if you will give me six hundred kilos for five million."

"Very impressive! I think that you are doing an amazing job. Here is what I'm going to do for you. I'm going to give you seven hundred kilos for the five, if you give me your word that you will spend at least fifteen million on your next trip," he responded.

I smiled and said, "I think that I can definitely do that with no problem."

My guys dropped the bags of money near Mr. Martinez's feet, and he signaled for one of his men to go and fill our order. While we were waiting, I told him about the botched robbery that took place before we came.

He told me that greed is a powerful thing, and that it was wise of me to assemble a solid crew because it takes a team to be truly successful in this game. Then he laughed and said, "I see that you're disguised as movers. I love your sense of humor, naming your company Move More."

Everyone laughed.

After we were loaded and ready to go, Martinez pulled me to the side and said, "I have some connections with the law enforcement community on your end. So today I'm going to make some calls and get you added to the protection list. I will email you some names of judges, detectives, and prosecutors, and I'll tell them to be expecting contributions from your family." He shrugged his shoulders and said, "It's the cost of doing business."

I told him thanks, and that I had no problem whatsoever contributing. The trip back was successful, and we now sat in the living area of our farmhouse.

I began giving disclosures of my recent decision. "Okay, everybody, since we have somewhere bigger, we will use the warehouse for storage and cooking. Teela, I want you to lace the place up with cameras and set up security. Tomorrow night, we are going to celebrate at Club Nitrous, so, Teela, wear something that will kill it. I don't care if it costs you twenty grand, and make sure that Tiny Tim, Cambright, and Rambeezy are there because I want to talk some business while we're there, assuming Mr. Joe lets us use his private office."

The crew just nodded their heads yes and tried their best to keep Teela's big surprise a secret. But I could tell they were excited.

The next day, I checked with Mr. Joe to see if everything was in order. When I got to the club, I saw Teela's name lit up across the front of the building, and it looked great.

I met Mr. Joe inside, busily working with the crew he had hired to set up Teela's private spot. Everything was done very tastefully. I was impressed.

When he saw me, he came over and said, "Well everything will be just like you wanted. Also I took the liberty of hiring seven new girls and a couple more bartenders. They will be wearing new uniforms with the logo Club Teela printed on them. The bar is fully stocked with backup in the storage area. Also I have bottles of high-end bubbly on deck for Teela's spot. The rap group are set to go on at eleven o'clock. Oh, don't forget to have Teela swing by the bank to finish her side of the paperwork."

"Wow! My man Joe! I knew you were the man to get everything done. It looks like club manager agrees with you more than being owner," I replied.

He laughed, then said, "It's a lot more fun when you don't have to worry about money s———t. I just might postpone my retirement for a while."

"Well you got a job here for as long as you want it," I said. Then I left to go and check on the progress of our warehouse being converted into another cooking facility.

Teela was all business when I walked in on her giving instructions to the workers she had hired. When she noticed me, she walked up to me, gave me a kiss, and said, "In a few more hours, everything will be done. Tiny Tim, Cambright, and Rambeezy are moving plates like hotcakes, especially Ram. But that is to be expected because he has the lowest prices."

"Well hold off on dropping the dirt off to Wilbrooks until tomorrow morning because he has some papers that he needs you to sign, and it's time for you to hire yourself a couple of assistants, just make sure that they are computer literate. Also make sure that they come and see me before they start. They will be representing FMB, so they need to be some bad b———tches. After you get done over here, meet me at the farm so we can get ready for our party tonight," I told her as I slapped her on her apple-shaped ass. "Tonight I will be wearing all white, all silk everything, so I want you to wear white as well!" I yelled back at her.

She nodded as I walked out.

The mood was festive at the farm as we all got ready for Teela's big night. I wore a Gucci suit with the shoes to match, plus I wore both of my FMB and lion head piece and chains. The crew, as usual, all wore black but in their own individual styles.

Teela stole the show when she came down the stairs in a skin-tight all-white designer bodysuit accentuating her sexy curves, and she had diamond-sprinkled high heels. Her makeup was professionally done, as was her hair, which was now cut in a mohawk with her name, Teela, on one side.

We all started cheering as she descended.

"Oooh weee, man! Them hoes are going to hate and love you at the same time!" I exclaimed.

Everyone started laughing when Tugga said, "True that!"

We drove away from the farm with me and Teela sandwiched in the middle of the two black SUVs. I knew that my Benz truck would stand out with it being all white. The club's parking lot was popping and packed to full capacity.

I took her hand and escorted her into the super crowded club, heading for her private section. When she looked at Queen of the North and her throne, she gave me a hug and a kiss. She then whispered into my ear, "Who says that dreams don't come true? Thank you so much, baby."

"For all that you do for our family, this is a token of our appreciation. So thank you, queen," I told her as I led her to her seat. The crowd went wild when they found out who was now running the North.

The Northside Head Busters took the stage and turned up as we popped bottles in our section. Free drinks was a hit because the twenty admittance charge was genius. Everyone in the place was having an awesome time. I motioned for Teela, Tim, Cambright, and Rambeezy to meet me in Teela's new office to discuss business.

When we went into the office, I explained to the heads of respective regions that I wanted them to add at least twenty more soldiers apiece to their squads. The reason was because I was upping each of their inventory to four thousand zones every two weeks, and that they would all be receiving another gun shipment just in case some regulating was needed. They all received new drop-off points to deposit money.

After we concluded, Teela and I went and danced in her private section, enjoying the rest of the night. Everyone now knew who was running the streets. When we were all partied out, I ordered the boys to escort me and Teela back to the farm.

As we started walking out, the crowd began chanting, "Teela, Teela, Teela!"

Teela smiled and waved goodbye.

Once we were inside the truck, she kissed me deeply, then said, "Slim, this was the night of all nights. I will cherish it for the rest of my days, baby."

"Then that means I did my job well because that's exactly what I was aiming for. But, baby girl, we are far from the finish line. We have an extraordinary amount of work left to do because my field of vision is widening, and you are a very important and intricate part of it. I love the way that you have executed all my commands in such a flawless manner from the very beginning, proving how irreplaceable you are. Plus you have some of the best p——ssy on the planet," I laughed and replied.

"Oh yeah? It's going to be all over your face tonight!" she remarked as the sounds of her musical laughter echoed inside the truck.

When we reached the farm, the boys went back to the club, but we ran upstairs and stripped our clothes off. Three hours went by as we brought intense pleasure to each other's body.

Finally, we laid back and talked business. "Baby girl, after you go and see Wilbrooks in the morning, I want you to work on finding the assistants that you need, and I will go and holler at Adam the Arab and place an order for a million dollars in guns that will be distributed to all four regions. Then I'm going to go and talk to Karen about her adding a couple more lawyers to our team. So while you're at Wilbrooks, add an extra million to her account," I told her.

She kissed me, then climbed on top of me, impaling herself on my stiffness. "I just love the way your mind works. Can you feel how wet and hot it makes my p——ssy feels?" she asked as she placed both of her hands on my chest and rotated her hips in a slow and meticulous manner.

I nodded and thought to myself if this wasn't heaven, it was damn close.

I woke up the next morning and found myself alone in the bed. That meant that Teela was off and running. I could hear echoes of laughter coming from downstairs. I washed my face, brushed my teeth, then headed down to meet everybody.

When Cutter saw me, he yelled, "There he goes! The boss of all bosses!"

"Hell yeah! Slim, last night was lit as f——k," said Tugga.

I smiled as I walked over to the coffee pot and poured myself a cup. I looked outside at the horses through the huge window and asked, "Does anyone know where we can get some good guard dog?"

Big Mosses said that he knew of a kennel out in Archer that carried top-of-the-line pit bulls and Rottweilers. I told him that I was thinking more along the lines of Dobermans. He said that the same people could maybe recommend a place and would see to it.

I sat down with my steaming cup of coffee and placed a call to Adam. I gave him destinations for the drop-off of my order and told him that my people would be down directly with his money and to pick up our portion of the order. He thanked me for the business and assured me that everything would get handled. I sent Lil "G" and Smoke to meet with him. Next, I called Karen and set a meeting with her for one o'clock, then I went upstairs to take a shower and get ready for the day.

I jumped into my white ghost and headed toward the hood. When I turned on Alcorn Street in the middle of the hood, I backed in and parked at Adam's corner store.

With my music banging like I was kicking up a concert, I watched as everyone migrated toward my truck, admiring how lit it was.

Finally, I decided to get down. Lil niggas came up to me and said, "Louisiana Slim, you holding it down for real, for real."

I laughed and said, "If y'all want to get money like me, get with Tugga and tell him that I said put y'all to work for FMB." I reached into my pocket and gave them a couple of hundreds apiece.

They thanked me as I walked inside the store to get some smokes.

When Adam looked my way, I asked, "Is business good?"

He smiled and said, "Sure is. As a matter of fact, I just concluded my end of a very lucrative deal."

"That's great! You do know that I wouldn't mind taking this store off your hands if you ever decided to sell," I hit back.

He began laughing and said, "No, no, no, this store is my bread and butter, not to mention my lifeline to the streets."

I laughed as I walked out of the door to find Valencia standing next to my truck.

Chapter 21

We rolled up slowly in front of the crowd of onlookers, whose eyes were on our little entourage. Cutter drove for us, so he got out after all the boys were standing in front of our truck, and opened the back door for us.

The crowd went crazy when they saw how ghetto-fabulous we looked. Teela looked up at the glitzy new sign displaying her name on the front of the building. Standing motionless in a state of shock as reality sat in, she placed both of her hands over her mouth like she was trying her best to stifle a scream.

She looked at all the smiling faces of our family with tears in her eyes and said, "I love."

Chapter 22

"What's up, stranger? I hear that you have been a very busy young man," she said, laughing as she removed her glasses.

After the initial shock wore off, I said, "Yeah, I've been getting it out the mud. It's been awhile since I've seen you, so what's popping?"

"Well Teela wanted me to come and do an interview with you before she gave me a job. So where are you going?" she asked.

That damn Teela is full of surprises, I thought as I opened the door and told Valencia to get in.

When she got inside, she said, "Damn, Slim, it looks like you've been making some major moves."

"I will tell you all about it when we get back at the farm."

We rode in comfortable silence. Twenty minutes later, we arrived at the farm. We got down and went inside to my office to find Teela sitting behind my desk.

She looked at me and said, "Oh, I see Valencia found you. Did you give her your approval?"

We sat down and I said, "We didn't get to that part yet. Did Valencia tell you about our history?" I asked.

"Yeah, she told me how you were supposed to marry her one day but just seemingly disappeared into thin air, so she continued her schooling and earned her business degree. So naturally, I thought that she would be a welcomed addition to our family," Teela responded.

I looked at Valencia who was enjoying me being in an uncomfortable position and asked, "Did Teela tell you about me and her?"

"Yeah, Romeo, she sure did," said Valencia.

"So what now?" I asked them both.

Teela walked up to Valencia, hugged her, smiled, and said, "Nigga, you better eat your wheaties because you have two wives now."

They began laughing.

Teela then said, "Hold the fort down because I'm taking Valencia shopping for a new wardrobe, a car, and on to Trust One to open her an account for $150,000. Oh, we're paying off all her student debts. Do you have a problem with any of that?" she asked, smiling and still hugging Valencia.

"No, but I think we're going to need a bigger bed," I remarked.

They laughed as they walked up to me and each gave me a kiss, then started walking toward the door. But before they walked out, I yelled, "Teela!"

When she looked back, I said, "Thank you."

She looked at me as seriousness crept into her eyes and said, "We both love you, so it was a no-brainer."

Then they left.

I sat alone and thought what had just happened. Life can be so beautiful but so complex in its simplicity.

Karen's secretary showed me to her office. She smiled and asked, "How is my favorite client? You know, I've made more money working for you than I actually do fighting court cases. Now I assume that you have big plans in mind, considering my recently inflated account."

"Yeah, I know that you have us covered on the criminal side of things, but now I need you to add a couple of contractual and business lawyers that are trustworthy and competent to our team. I'm ready to start my own company in real estate development. You see, Karen, my family has grown immensely and so has our income potential. Now we need a way to become established in the mainstream economy. Therefore, my thoughts veered toward real estate," I told her.

She looked at me with serious eyes and said, "Thomas, I love your ambition, and I think that this is a great move. I have just the right lawyers in mind. Actually, they are brothers who are exceptionally smart. I call them the Johnson Boys. But you're going to need a building for your new company, so should I begin a search for one that's on the market?" she asked.

"Yes, because I want this project done as fast as humanly possible. I want the name of the company to be FMB Developments. I'm thinking we can spend a couple million on the building and another three on equipment and supplies," I replied.

She got up and shook my hand and said, "That type of money moves mountains and magically dissolves red tape, so give me a couple of months, and everything will be done."

I thanked her and then went back to the farm where Rambeezy was waiting for me.

"What's up, Slim? I have a little problem on my hands. There is a detective by the name of Gilbert who came to see me about getting paid to stay out of our way," he told me.

"What kind of numbers was he talking about?" I asked.

"S——t! That boy was talking about $10,000 a month," responded Rambeezy.

"Well tell him that your boss wants to meet with him at our favorite Mexican restaurant, and that he should bring whoever else that's interested in working for us. Tell him he will see me sitting with two women in the back corner at four o'clock," I instructed.

When I got upstairs, the girls were back, and they were trying on outfits and laughing.

Teela walked up to me, kissed me, and asked, "What have you been up to?"

"You know me, just doing a little shaking and baking. Speaking of which, I need you both to be dressed and ready for a meeting at the restaurant at four. Valencia may as well see how we do things. Valencia, you are a boss now, so I hope that you are ready because we're trying to do big things. I have big plans for you. We will get stupid rich and have fun. But we have to work hard to make it happen. I see that you're wearing the family crest around your neck. Did Teela school you on what it means to be a part of this family?" I asked.

She walked up to me and looked me in the eyes as she began unzipping my pants, saying, "Loyalty and willingness to bust my gun for you." As she fondled my member, she kneeled down, smiled, and said, "Now are you willing to bust your gun for me?" Then she took my stiffness into her deliciously hot mouth.

Teela laughed and said, "Valencia, you are one bad b——tch!" Then she joined the fun.

A couple of hours later, we were headed toward the restaurant. Cutter drove us as we all sat inside the back of the white ghost. We got out and went inside to the back table. Cutter sat at another table with a duffle bag containing $200,000.

Both Teela and Valencia sat in suspense as we all waited. When they heard the sound of the bell signaling new arrivals, Teela stared at the six men coming through the door.

Three detectives and three uniformed officers made up the little band of men. They walked up to our table and yelled, "Freeze!"

Chapter 23

Detective Gilbert smiled, then put out his hand for a shake, and said "I'm just kidding" as the rest of his guys laughed.

I offered him a seat and introduced him to the girls. Then I explained that as long as he and his guys remained loyal to our family, they would always be taken cared for. I motioned for Cutter to come over with the bag of money.

Looking at Gilbert, I said, "There are $200,000 in that bag. So I expect to keep both you and your guys paid at the $10,000 a month rate until the money run out. When that happens, you will get with Ms. Valencia here for future payments. It goes without saying that I want any information on anyone who are not of the FMB family who are trying to make big money moves. Other than that, I would like to welcome you boys to the family."

I shook their hands, and they departed.

When they were gone, Valencia said, "Wow, so we're operating outside of the designated rules? Like a world inside of a world?"

"Yeah, you're beginning to catch on. Slim creates his own reality while altering our realities along with his. He wants and sees a bigger and better future for us all, and the genius of it all is that anyone who helps him to achieve his goals will win in a way that they have never won before. So it may seem like he's spreading around too much money but just consider the vision that he's bringing into being. Me myself believed in him from the start, even before I fell in love with him. He is definitely one of a kind. He doesn't value money but understands the fundamental value of money and its application in reference to problem-solving. So I can't wait to see where this journey takes us all," responded Teela.

"Hmm, I'm beginning to understand, and since seeing is believing, I too believe," remarked Valencia.

I sat in silence as these two beautiful women talked of me in such a wonderous light that it was, I don't know, fascinating somehow.

I looked at Teela and asked, "How much dirt have we accumulated since the last trip?"

"Twenty-eight million and counting plus another six that's cleaned and ready for use. Now that the whole state is ours, we're making more money than the casinos," she replied.

Valencia's eyes widened as she asked, "Is that really the kind of capital that this family has?"

"Now you can see why I went MIA on you. We had to turn nothing into something."

"Now it's all about keeping what we've worked so hard for and balancing all the bad with an equal amount of good because everybody knows that karma is a b———tch," I told Valencia.

Teela looked at me and said, "Well it's been nice chilling with y'all, but I have some club business that I need to handle, so I'll catch up with y'all at the house." She got up, kissed me, then she kissed Valencia and said, "I'm so happy that we have another getting put in power. FMB for life!" Then she walked out, leaving us alone.

Valencia stared at Teela as she walked out, then said, "I can see why you have her. She's amazing. I just hope that I can measure up."

I took her hands into mine and said, "There is no competition in this family, only the need to thrive as a whole, and that applies even in our bedroom. Straight talk, I'm not always available to appease you or her sexually. So don't be adverse to exploring with Teela because we are now one. Can you dig that?"

Valencia smiled and said, "Well she is a very beautiful option. I'll keep that in mind. Do you know if she's treaded those particular waters before, or are you sending me on a mission?" Then started laughing.

I stood up and said, "I think that you are a perfect fit for our family. Let's go home, so I can bring you up to speed on a few plans I had in motion."

Valencia was awestruck by all that we were able to accomplish thus far. I told her that I needed her to learn all she could about real estate development, and that a crash course would be needed because I was planning on making her a CEO in a couple of months.

"CEO of what?" she asked.

"Well it's top secret, but I plan on surprising the family by having us own our own company. It's going to be called FMB Developments. So far, I've put four million into it, but I expect to spend at least ten more, which is where you come in at. It will be your job to oversee the spending of this ten-million-dollar budget. So staffing, supplies, computers, and vehicles are yours to obtain for us. I need you to try and catapult our family into legitimacy. Once we've reached that level, we will direct our forces at helping our people who are poverty stricken," I told her.

"Wow! I had no idea that you harbored such aspirations. The task is daunting, but with a ten-million-dollar budget, my job will be easier. I only have to delegate and supervise. Now I fully understand what Teela said about your vision." She kissed me and said, "I think I'm falling in love with you all over again." Then she laughed.

"So what kind of car did you get?" I asked.

"I got an all-black Lexus coupé, modest and elegant at the same time," she responded.

I told her it was a nice choice as I took her clothes off.

Teela came home and found us both asleep. She took a shower and jumped into the bed beside me and fell into a deep sleep.

I must have sensed her presence because I woke up the next morning with my arms wrapped around her. I sneaked out of bed while they both slept and went downstairs to find the crew getting ready for the day.

Big Mosses asked me if I wanted to go outside and see the dogs that he got for us. I told him that I did, and we went out back to the miniature kennel that had been erected.

"Nice! I see that you've been busy, huh?" I asked.

"Yeah, the dogs are top of the line, and they are really smart. Their names are Star and Killer," he remarked.

The dogs were very healthy looking with shiny coats. They took to me very quickly, and before I knew it, they were following me around. I checked up on the cattle and saw that we now had a few calves in the mist. The cowhands were doing a great job.

Mosses wanted to talk business. He told me that he had this cousin who lived in Michigan where zones went for $2,000 apiece.

I looked at him and said, "Really?"

My wheels were churning.

Chapter 24

"Sounds like this could be something worthwhile. Let me make a call and see if I can secure us a home down there so we can set up shop. If Wilbrooks can find something, I want you to go down there with a team of ten soldiers and ten hustlers. Stay for a month and see what it do. I'll send you there with eight thousand zones. Let's go inside so I can let Teela know that she may be losing you for a while," I told him.

"Boss, I don't think that she will like that!" Big Mosses said and chuckled.

"S——t! I know she won't like it, but she'll chill once she realizes the potential," I replied.

*****

"You wanna what! Why not let Lil 'G' go up there and run it since he's next up for a promotion?" asked Teela after I told her of the new plans.

"Because it's Mosses's blood kin who will be familiarizing us with the streets out there, and if things go like I think they will, Lil 'G', Tugga, and Cutter will be heading out there with their own crew. They will each run an appointed region the same way we're running this state. I'm ready for a hostile takeover if them niggas try to buck the system, but I doubt that will happen because making s——tloads of money kills beef. With that in mind, I'll set the prices at $1,000 a zone if two is what they're now, which is a great price for us and them. The zones will fly off the shelves for that price at a superfast rate. Mosses, what region does your people live in?" I asked.

"It's the South region, boss," he replied.

"Well, Teela, let Wilbrooks know that we need something live-in ready in an isolated location in the South. How much time are we playing with before our next trip to Martinez?" I asked.

"One month because this state's appetite is insatiable. You may want to think about spending at least thirty million if you plan on supplying two states," Teela told me.

"Nah, more like fifty. That way, I could get a better deal. I'm thinking something like five thousand kilos for fifty million, which would actually amount to ten thousand kilos using our come up formula," I told her.

"Baby, we could easily net two hundred million or more with that kind of inventory. See, Valencia, this nigga got plans inside of plans," Teela said, and we all started laughing.

"Slim, exactly what is the extent of your education? Because it's astounding the way you think and move," asked Teela.

I laughed and said, "Only one year of college, majoring in philosophy!"

Then everyone laughed again.

"Valencia, I want you to go and see Karen, our lawyer, and she will introduce you to the two new lawyers who will be working with you on your project. Tell Karen the capacity in which you will be working. Get an update on the progress of things and allocate any funds that Karen may need out of your budget. I'll call Wilbrooks and let him know that you are to have access to the said amount we discussed earlier. Report back to me when you're finished," I instructed.

"Okay, baby, I'm going to go and get myself together and be off," she replied.

Teela looked at me and said, "I don't even want to guess what you have her working on, but I'm sure it's going to be something that we can't fathom."

"It's just something to keep her busy and not feel left out," I told her as I headed upstairs and got into bed. Deep sleep overcame me.

I woke up a few hours later and received a progress report from Valencia on our company's upstart.

"Well Karen has found us a great building that was once an insurance place with extended property for equipment and supplies, but I had to take three mil out of the budget to complete the deal. Also I talked to the Johnson brothers, and they are wonderfully smart and super capable. They have just about gotten all the paperwork done, so next week, you will be needed to sign the respective papers, finalizing everything and bringing the company to life. Contractors have been hired to put *FMB Developments* in huge bold lettering across the front of the building at a cost of $700,000 but it's worth it. I'm working on a deal to procure transport vehicles and proper equipment. All in all, I think that we are moving at an extraordinary pace. Staff will begin in a couple of weeks, and we will be working hand in hand with Conrad's Real Estate. So that's where we are right now. Any questions or further instruction for me?" Valencia asked.

"Yes. I want you to hire minorities for the bulk of your staff and make sure it's predominantly women and invest in good advertisements. That's all for now," I said as I kissed her.

Teela walked in while I was kissing Valencia and said, "Y'all are still playing mommy and daddy in here?" Then she started laughing.

I got up and walked toward the door as I said, "Hell to the no! I got business, so y'all can play with each other for a change."

Teela looked at Valencia and said, "We could do that."

I closed the door on the two kissing beauties.

A couple of hours later, Teela found me downstairs watching the news channel on our huge flatscreen. She let me know that Wilbrook had found us a nice set up spot in Michigan. So I told her to get with Mosses and arrange a flight for his cousin so I could talk with him ASAP.

"Teela, make preparations for transport, product placement, and guns and send five cookers along and give them extra relocation pay," I ordered.

"Right away!" she replied and left.

Big Mosses looked at me and said, "Man, I will miss being out here at the farm, but I know that we have to keep grinding."

"Yeah, big man. Grinding is the only way we can keep this money machine running, and we will miss having you around here as well. FMB for life," I said as I gave him a hug.

Chapter 25

The young cat who went by the name of Grip was a suave-looking character, standing almost as tall as I did. He dressed with that hip-hop flare that most youngsters were rocking.

Big Mosses made the introductions when he, Teela, and Grip entered my office.

"How was your flight?" I asked once we were all seated.

"The flight was lit! First class is the way to go. I wasn't expecting that. My big cuz told me y'all were making moves, but I didn't know y'all were coming like that!" he replied.

"Yeah, we are a very established and successful organization. Now I want you to give me a rundown on the state of things in the streets out there," I countered.

"Well the prices are so high because nobody has a real plug, so nobody is supplying the streets like that. Just a few niggas here and there, getting their hands on some work and selling it sky high. You know, supply and demand type of s——t. It's really wide open for someone with major product to come and take over the market," was his response.

I looked at Teela and said, "I want the guys on the road within the next forty-eight hours. Grip, you will work directly with Mosses, connecting him with buyers who want some weight, and you will receive $50,000 with the option of hustling for our family once we get established out there. Teela, send five kilos along with the allotted eight thousand zones so the cookers will have some work. Mosses, I want you to check out each region once you get established so we can send Cutter, Lil 'G', and Tugga out to those parts with their own crew. Am I missing anything, Teela?" I asked.

"Well I think we should get Karen to get on her lawyer s——t and find us a great criminal lawyer out there to get added to the team. Plus get Johnny the Jeweler to work his magic and make some more crest chains with the letter M standing out in green stones since the new members will be from Michigan because we will no doubt do some recruiting out there. But other than that, I think you've covered all the bases."

"Okay, good thinking," I remarked as Valencia walked into the office and asked, "Are we going out tonight or what?"

Teela smiled and said, "Actually, that's a great idea. This will be Mosses's last time partying with us for a while, plus we can show li'l Michigan how we do it in the South."

I laughed and said, "Okay, that's a wrap. Let everybody know we're going out tonight. Teela and Valencia y'all come with me and take a ride through the hood."

We took the white ghost with me, Tugga in the front, and the girls in the back. I looked over at Tugga and said, "Pretty soon you will be relocating to Michigan with your own crew. Are you ready for that?" I asked.

"Hell yeah! I've been watching and learning from the best. You and Teela are like street professors," he exclaimed, and we all started laughing.

As we descended into the heart of the hood, poverty became more pronounced. The homes took on a shabby quality. *But the people were strong in their acceptance of their situation as they fought for everything they had*, I thought.

The thought of affordable subdivisions for minorities began to consume my mind. *What if I strengthen the core with provision for better educational advantages for these low-income students trying to climb out of the gutter? Yeah, as soon as FMB Developments is off and running, I will be tackling real-life problems through our company's veneer*, I thought. This company was going to change a lot of lives.

I pulled up to the old house where I used to live and saw Brenda and Troy sitting on the big shaded porch, drinking beer. I saw the huge smile cover Brenda's face when we got down.

Brenda ran toward me and hugged me and said, "Slim, it's so good to see you! I guess you've been pretty busy, huh?"

Before I could answer, Tugga said, "Slim has only one gear, go!"

We all started laughing.

"Can a nigga get a beer?" I asked.

"Slim, you can have anything you want. Who's the new girl with Mrs. Teela?" she asked.

Teela smiled and said, "She's his other wife. He's got the both of us now. Valencia, meet Brenda. She's been holding it down with us from day one."

The two women shook hands, and Valencia told Brenda that it was nice to meet her.

We sat next to Troy, and I asked him how were things going. He told me that their lives had changed for the better ever since I had stepped into their yard that long time ago.

We chilled with them for a couple of hours, catching up on street gossip and listening to Brenda tell stories about them being the first Whites to live in a Black neighborhood.

Brenda laughed and said, "They used to whip Troy's ass every time somebody got busted by the cops because they thought he was an undercover cop or something. After about his eighth ass whupping, he finally learned how to fight back. Now they say we act more like niggas than they do!"

We laughed until tears rolled down our faces.

Finally, I got up and said, "Well it's been nice, but we have to go and get ready for a party at Club Teela tonight. If you and Troy want to roll with us, I can send a car to pick y'all up, and Teela can give y'all the VIP treatment."

"Hell yeah, we want to come! We heard that Mrs. Teela owned a club now unless y'all fooling us again, and it's you, Slim, who owns it," she remarked.

I laughed and said, "Not this time. Teela is the sole owner. Y'all's ride will be here at ten. Teela, hit them up with twenty rack so they can upgrade their ride."

Brenda jumped up and down and yelled, "Thank you so much! FMB is the s———t!"

We all laughed as we climbed into the white ghost and headed back to the farm.

When we were back home in our room, Valencia said, "Those people were great. It's been a long time since I've laughed like that, Slim. They love you to death. I have no doubt that they would bust their guns for you without hesitation. This is truly an amazing family that you've created, and I'm proud to be a part of it."

"Sky's the limit!" I replied as we continued to get ready.

Chapter 26

I shut down our whole operation for the night and had ordered the entire FMB family to attend Big Mosses's going away party. Even the cookers and stable hands were invited. Teela and Valencia wore matching outfits, looking like Amazon sisters. I sent Smoke in my black truck to pick Brenda and Troy up.

We departed from the farm, heading out to the club. The parking lot was packed as usual. I hadn't been at the club since opening night.

When Teela, Valencia, and I got out of the white ghost, the crowd started cheering like we were stars. We entered the club and headed toward Teela's private spot. I stopped dead in my tracks when I saw a king's throne with a chair on either side of it for both Teela and Valencia. Each chair carried one of the letters of our family's acronym.

I looked down at the smiling Teela. "Now whose full of surprises?" I asked as I gave them each a kiss.

Teela whispered, "You are our king, baby."

The FMB family were about a hundred deep.

Valencia said, "Wow! I didn't know that we had these many members."

"Yeah, we're growing at a fast rate, and everybody is eating," I told her.

Teela grabbed the mic and yelled, "Anytime Slim comes to the club, all drinks are free all night long!"

Everybody cheered.

We partied hard in our section with both Brenda and Troy seated with us.

Brenda yelled, "Y'all, be doing it big in this b——tch! Thanks for letting us roll."

I nodded at her.

A couple of hours later, I sent a text to all the heads, telling them to meet me in Teela's office.

When they walked in, they all smelled and looked like new money. After we greeted one another, they took a seat.

"I just wanted to update you all on what's going on. We are about to take over Michigan, and Big Mosses here is a boss now. He will pioneer the expansion. We will start the operation in the South region, but explore the other regions for a complete takeover. That means Cutter, Lil 'G', and Tugga will become bosses of their own crews as well. Also I will soon be unveiling a new project that boss lady Valencia is working on for the family.

Now are there any issues that need to be addressed in any region?" I asked.

"Well business is booming on my end to a point that I need more product added to my regular shipments, but other than that, we're good on my end," said Cambright.

"Cool, that's not a problem. That's good news. So, Teela, double up on everybody's supply," I ordered.

Teela passed everyone a drink, and we toasted good luck to Mosses. Then we headed back to the party.

Hours later, as I lay naked in the bed with the girls smoking a cigarette, I said, "Valencia, I want you to buy us a limo and hire a driver. The color I want is cream with butter pecan interior. Oh, make sure it's a Rolls-Royce."

"Damn!" Teela squealed. "We're upgrading in this b——tch!"

"Yeah, but no more spending until we get back with the next shipment, I hope. Teela, you will still have to get another assistant because Valencia is too f——cking overqualified, plus she's heading an entire operation at the moment," I told her.

Teela looked at me and said, "Okay, what gives? What's up with this secret operation!"

"Okay, okay! Don't tell the rest of the family yet, but we are about to own our own company. It's going to be called FMB Developments. Valencia is going to be the CEO," I finally told her.

Teela smiled and said, "Damn, baby! That's awesome. Just think about all the jobs we can create, and the huge amount of people that we can help. Plus the moneys from the company will automatically cleanse itself. How much are we putting into it?" she asked.

"It's costing us a lot, but it's worth it. The building and properties was 7.7 million plus another ten million to get proper equipment, vehicles, supplies, computers, and staffing, and we have two more lawyers on the team called the Johnson brothers. Valencia has been instructed to hire mostly from the minority pool and female gender because I feel it's time for women to rise to power. Our company will reflect how our family highly values women and respect your abilities. Valencia, our first order of business will be to create low-cost, beautiful subdivisions for families who never had s——t. People who can never get a break in this hard life.

"Then we will go over to the high schools and create full scholarship programs for low-income students because poverty shouldn't stop a person from excelling," I ended.

Valencia leaned over and kissed me, then said, "I believe in you, Slim."

Then Teela kissed me. "We're about to f——k you, silly, because I know that both of our p——ssies are wet right now!" she exclaimed, and we laughed as they attacked me.

The next morning, I was chilling, watching the news when Grip entered the room.

"Slim, I had big fun last night. Y'all go hard as f——k in the South. Man, I'm happy to be affiliated with FMB."

I smiled and said, "It's easy to get rich f——cking with us. *All you have to do is follow orders, remain loyal, and never question nothing I say, and definitely do not steal from us because that will end your career."

His eyes widen as he said, "I understand. Any nigga would be crazy to try some foul s——t like that, knowing how deep your numbers are. It looked like I saw an FMB member everywhere I looked last night."

"Yeah, we have big numbers and big guns, and everybody is down to bust his gun for the family. We rich crazy niggas," I told him and laughed.

A few hours later, the transport truck and supplies, along with everyone who were leaving for Michigan, arrived. We said our goodbyes and wished Big Mosses luck once again. Then the girls and I watched as they all pulled away from the farm.

Chapter 27

When we went back inside, Teela said, "It feels like a son leaving home for college or something."

"I know what you mean. It's the same feeling I got when Rambeezy left to go and run the South side, but it's inevitable because expansion is a must if we want to keep soaring. Accomplishing big things comes at a certain price. But us living in total comfort and having the ability to help others on a large scale are worth the sacrifice."

Valencia walked in and asked me if she was going with us on the next trip.

"Yes, you are, but this will be the last time any of us make a trip out there. The fact is we are too important in this come up process to be taking unnecessary chances. That's why we're leaving three hours ahead of transport," I remarked.

A couple of weeks later, the girls and I took a ride out to the company building to check out our new sign.

Teela looked up at the sign and said, "Wow! It's really happening. It all seems so surreal. I can still remember when Slim got Tugga, Lil 'G', Rambeezy, and me together at his old house where Brenda and Troy now lives. He asked us if we wanted to work for him. I mean we four were barely making ends meet. We didn't even know Slim had it like that. Once he sold us on his vision and we agreed to work for him, he gave each of us a duffle bag that he called balling kits. Each bag contained twenty-five zones, a cell phone, five thousand in cash, and a gun.

"*All* he asked for was loyalty, ability to follow orders, and willingness to bust our guns for one another. Once we were all done selling our product, he let us keep all the money and still paid us for selling it! Can you believe it? I asked him why, and he said because we followed orders."

Valencia laughed and said, "Slim has the uncanny ability to make others really see the importance of smaller things that when connected becomes something huge. You do know that we are two of the luckiest b——tches on the planet?"

Teela said, "Yes, ma'am, we are, and you can bet that he loves us both equally, which in itself is amazing."

Valencia hugged Teela and said, "I love you too, Teela."

Teela smiled and said, "And I love your big fine ass too. Now let's go and work on getting his private office on the top floor done up boss style."

"Yeah, then we can work on our own offices once we're finished."

*****

"Things are on schedule, and my girls and I should be paying you a visit in a few days," I said to Martinez.

"Good! I will be expecting you. I can't wait to get updated on your progress. I'm really beginning to enjoy your story. It's been a hell of a ride for you. At one time, I thought that Big Boi was going to have your kind of success, but he became complacent. But he is very loyal, so I keep him onboard. There is no substitute for it," replied Martinez.

"Yeah, I feel the same way exactly. Well I will be seeing you soon," I told him, then hung up.

The girls came back, and they looked like they were up to something, but I didn't ask what. Instead, I told them of my talk with Martinez.

"Boy, is he going to be surprised when we go this time because we've been really getting it and making more money than we've ever made," responded Teela.

"Yeah, Martinez is a real player ass nigga in his own way. He's supersmart and easy to get along with, but I suspect he's done more dirt than us to get where he's at right now. Remember how he tried to get me to work for him the first time we met? Trying to give me all them kilos on consignment. That showed me that he knows how to exploit opportunities for personal gain when he sees it. I have a feeling that if I had gone for that deal, FMB would now be working for him. But he had me f——cked up because I wasn't trying to be under him but more like him. I'm a self-made boss, so why lose that freedom for the greed of money? But I do respect his power, and now I think he respects mine," I replied.

"That's a great point. Because of you not falling for that pot of gold, we can now move at our pace and not answer to anyone about anything. Now look at us. We're doing things that we never thought were possible. Do you realize how much money we will be bringing in once we have complete control of Michigan's market? S——t! We could actually invest in having our own small bank!" Teela said and laughed.

A light bulb went off in my head as I looked at Teela and said, "Pretty girl, that's not a bad idea. We could call it the People's Bank, and we could steal Wilbrooks from Trust One Bank to run it for us. It would eliminate our cleaning cost, and instead, we could clean other people's money if we choose to. Just imagine how many small businesses we could help get started for a certain percentage of equity. FMB would truly become connected and become a vital part of the community. Then we will have the power of the people behind us."

"Also the bank would become instantly successful by all the projects that FMB Developments runs through it. I mean, why let Trust One reap all the benefits? Plus we will be able to pour all our dirty moneys directly into our bank and never have to worry about accumulation problems ever again. It will be like us having our own personal giant safe," remarked Valencia.

I sat quietly for a few minutes, thinking, then said, "Okay, girls! That's what we're going to do. We will wait until after the big shipment so we can use the first seventy-five million to get our bank up and running. Now let's go get something to eat."

Chapter 28

A couple of weeks later, the girls and I went to our new company building. Everything looked great and up to date. They took me to the fourth floor to an office that I assumed was for Valencia, but when I opened the door, I was surprised to see the very masculine-looking interior. Mahogany-colored furnishing and burgundy leather—imported, no doubt—dominated the space. The chair behind the huge desk had *Louisiana Slim* stitched across the back of it. The view was great, and I noticed a picture with the three of us together on my desktop. I turned toward the girls, and they both yelled, "Surprise!"

I smiled and said, "I knew you two were up to something last week. I love it. Oh, I see adjoining doors on each sides."

"Yes, it just makes access easier, and it makes more sense for us all to work from here. I finally got myself a couple of assistants, and Valencia has her own secretary, so we're all set," Teela told me.

Valencia jumped in and said, "I'm almost through with staffing. When I'm finished, we will have over a hundred people working for us, doing various jobs to make this monster run smoothly. Inside six months, we will be employing even more, so this economy will get a great boost from us. Because of that, the mayor's office has been in touch with us and wants a meet with you in a couple of hours, so we're taking our limo so we can make a good impression."

"That's great because it will give us a chance to get in good with him, so tell our lawyers that I want them to drop everything that they're doing and meet us at Mayor Perkin's office in a couple of hours. Teela, make sure that everything is in order for our trip to

Martinez's tomorrow. We will be taking the limo on that trip too," I told them.

Teela smiled and said, "Things are coming together like cooking straight drop!"

We all laughed and went back to the farm so I could change for the big meeting.

Two hours later, I was shown into the mayor's office with my team. The red-faced, robust-looking Mr. Perkins jumped up from behind his desk and walked up to me with his hands out, "Mr. Thomas, I presume? I'm so happy that you could come because I know that you're busy getting your new company off the ground."

After shaking his hand, I introduced him to my team, and he offered us a seat.

He continued speaking, saying, "I just wanted to tell you that the city is behind you, and if there is anything that this office can do to help you, just let me know. After all, your company will help in raising our economic status. So are there any projects that you're interested in tackling?"

"Yes, our first project will be converting some of our accumulated properties into subdivision that will be affordable to low-income residents. Then we will be wanting to set up a full scholarship program as well for low-incomed and minority-based students. Our company will begin this program with two million dollars. I understand that it's getting close for reelection time?" I asked.

"As a matter of fact, it is!" he responded.

I smiled and said, "Well our company will be supporting you to the fullest, so you can expect a two hundred thousand contribution from us, and we will let you unveil the said projects, and you can also let the voters know that you influenced us to do so. That will, no doubt, win you the election in a landslide."

"Mr. Thomas, I think I need to hire you as my campaign manager!" he laughed. "I'm sure that we will do great things for this city," he said.

I looked at Teela and said, "Make sure that Mr. Perkins receives his contribution by the end of the business day."

"Now, Mr. Perkins, please excuse us because we have some very pressing business matters to attend to," I told him.

He shook my hand vigorously and said, "Thank you for the generous campaign contribution and the great idea on the format I'll be running on. Here is my personal number. If you ever encounter any type of trouble in the city limits, just give me a call, and I will take care of it immediately."

I thanked him, and we departed. I invited our lawyers to lunch at our favorite restaurant.

When we were finally seated, Karen said, "I can't believe how you had that hard-ass eating out of your hands like that."

Everyone laughed.

One of the Johnsons piped in, saying, "Mr. Thomas, you have a great business savvy. Maybe you should think about running for office one day."

"*Please*! Don't give him any more ideas!" Teela yelled, and the table erupted into peals of laughter.

Valencia took my hand and said, "Seriously though, I'm very proud of the way you handled yourself back there. You really represented the FMB family to the fullest. I still can't believe he gave you his personal number. Nobody better not mess with you in this city, or it will be off with their heads!"

More laughter came.

After we got through eating, we walked outside to our awaiting limo.

Karen said, "Wow! I love this car! It's so luxurious."

I told her that if she ever needed it for a special occasion, she should get with Valencia, and she would have the car and driver sent to her.

"Thank you, I just might take you up on that offer one day. Well it's back to the grind," she replied and walked away.

The girls and I headed home to make preparations for our big trip the next day. As we were pulling up to the farm, my cell went off. It was big Mosses.

"What it do, big man?" I asked.

"What's up, boss? I just wanted you to know that everything is on the up and up out here. Zones are moving faster here than it does back home. Them boys were thirsty for a plug. They're treating me with much respect. You can send the rest of the boys down when you get ready, and I'll help them set up," he reported.

"That's great news, Mosses!" I responded, then hung up.

"Was that Mosses?" Teela asked.

"Yeah, and he says business is better there than it is here. Imagine that," I said.

"Let's get that money then!" she squealed.

Chapter 29

The next day, the girls and I were in the limo, heading out to Martinez's house ahead of our transport team. We were enjoying the ride, sipping champagne and discussing business.

Teela said, "I knew that Mosses was going to do a great job down there. Now all we need is the rest of the guys to follow his lead if we really want to get a bank up and running. Have you discussed the possibility with Wilbrooks yet?"

"No, I haven't, but we still have some time before we embark on that venture. Don't worry about the other boys handling their business because they are more than ready to run their own crews."

Four hours later, we were entering my plug's estate. When we pulled up in front of Martinez's home, he was standing out front, waiting to greet us with a huge smile on his face. One of his guys opened the doors for us.

When Martinez saw both girls, his eyes widened. He gave me a hug and said, "Slim, it's good to see you. I see that you're riding in comfort and with lovely companions. Now that's how you travel."

"Yeah, we're on another level now. This is Valencia a new member of our family. When we get settled, I will explain in what capacity she works," I replied.

"Well then let us go inside and discuss business," he gestured.

Valencia was impressed with the inside as much as she was with the outside of his home and complimented Martinez on his taste.

When we were seated, his maid served us some drinks, then quietly slipped out of the room.

Martinez said, "As I recall, you gave me your word that you would be spending fifteen million this time. Are you able to do that?"

I smiled and said, "Actually, I'm here to spend fifty million."

"My, my! You are full of surprises. I must admit I wasn't expecting that. What do you want for the fifty?" he asked.

"Well I wanted you to give me five thousand kilos," I replied.

"I can do that, but why are you buying so much this time?" he asked.

I looked at Teela and said, "Why don't you give Mr. Martinez a rundown on what's been going on with the family since we last saw him."

She cleared her throat and said, "Since we last met, our family has decided to invest in legitimizing our name by starting our own company, and we started one called FMB Developments, employing over a hundred people. Valencia here is the CEO. We have the full support of the mayor whom we've given a sizeable campaign contribution to. We've started the process of a full scholarship program for low-income minority students, and we've expanded our horizons by planting our feet in Michigan. We expect to be supplying the entire state by the end of the month, and that is why we need our inventory on full tilt. This was all Slim's vision in our family's quest for stability."

Martinez looked at me with a twinkle in his eyes. "I just knew that I was about to hear some great things. You have accomplished so much in such a small amount of time. Do you ever sleep?" he asked and laughed.

Valencia said, "He doesn't get much because he still has to take care of both Teela and me."

We continued laughing.

"Well a toast is in order. To success!" Martinez said as he raised his glass.

"Success!" we countered.

The time seemed to melt as we enjoyed Martinez's company. Before we knew it, his people were telling him that our people had arrived and brought the money. After they packed up the kilos, they left while we stayed with Martinez a moment longer.

Martinez said, "It's hard to imagine all that you've done, but I get the feeling that you're just getting started. The most important thing is that you're doing it the right way. If everyone is being taken care of, they will do their part to make the money train never stops. It costs money to make money."

"Yeah! And I just want to thank you for helping with our family's rise to power. We have over one hundred soldiers and more guns than you can imagine. Big guns, big numbers, and loyalty give us a fighting chance at survival," I replied.

After a few more words, the girls and I departed.

When we were in the limo heading back home, Valencia told us that she thought that Martinez was very charming, and that maybe we should upgrade and build ourselves a home like or better than his. I told her that we would get around to it sooner or later.

A few hours later, we were all chilling at the farm, exhausted from the trip, but Teela left to go and make sure everything was put away properly and set into motion the distribution procedures. A couple of hours later, she returned, took a shower, got in the bed with us, and went straight to sleep.

The next day, we were up early inside our limo, heading to our offices. I sat behind my desk and admired the view as I placed calls to Tugga, Lil "G", and Cutter, ordering them down to the office dressed in suits.

An hour later, the three neatly dressed young men walked into my office.

Tugga looked around and said, "I can't believe that we have our own company! S———t, the sign outside is matching my chair. That's big, Slim."

"*All* this is because of all the hard work that we've put in. Now I want the three of you ready to relocate to Michigan to run your own crews. Y'all niggas are bosses now. You will start with ten soldiers, ten hustlers, and three cookers apiece. Tugga, you got the North, Lil 'G' has the East, and Cutter will run the West region. I will give y'all the addresses of your new homes when y'all leave this weekend. Mosses will help y'all get started. Any questions?" I asked.

When they told me that they were ready and understood everything, I dismissed them.

Then I sat, staring out the window, thinking about our future.

Chapter 30

By the time Friday came, the guys departure for Michigan, FMB Developments was fully staffed and working on its first subdivision home project. No farewell party was given this time because we were on a serious mission to build capital for the family's dream bank. There was a sense of urgency in everyone's movements.

We watched as our Michigan crew left to go and set up their perspective trap houses. Teela held my hand tightly as she whispered, "Good luck, guys."

I led both girls back into our home and said, "Okay, girls, we need to get ready for the mayor's campaign rally."

"With everything that's going on, I almost forgot that you're speaking today," said Teela.

"Yea, and even though the speech is designed to help make the mayor look good, it will help get the power of the people behind us. Money is nothing without it. I want FMB to become part of this community's fabric."

The rally was held in the heart of the downtown area, and there seemed to be thousands gathered for the event. We sat on the makeshift stage along with his other contributors who were awarded seats.

The mayor began his speech:

> Thank you all for coming and supporting me in my bid for reelection. I have worked hard to make this city safe and strong. I have especially concentrated copious amounts of energy and time improving our economic status, and because

of this, new businesses like FMB Developments and others have chosen our city as their home. Now I've had the pleasure of getting to know the owner of FMB Developments personally, and I've been able to influence him to build beautiful subdivisions for low-income families. Families who have lived in poverty but will not have the chance to live and raise their home in a structurally safe environment.

The crowd went crazy and started cheering.

When the cheers finally subsided, he continued, "We are also working together to create a full scholarship program, aiming at low-income students who will get a chance to go to college for free. All they have to do is work hard and make good grades. It's life changing because these students would normally not get a chance to attend a university."

The crowd cheered again.

Then the mayor said, "I would like you all to meet Mr. Thomas, owner of this wonderful company, who will now say a few words."

The crowd cheered as I walked up to the podium but got really quiet as I started speaking.

"The mayor has convinced me that economic growth is the only way that this city, our new home, will continue to thrive, and to make this happen, we have to work together to help those struggling a chance to be in position to participate in these efforts. Not only will these subdivisions be of great quality, but also each will house substation with security personnel working twenty-four hours a day to detour crime from coming near our kids. That way, the parents can concentrate on parenting and encouraging their kids to try and achieve higher goals. As long as FMB Developments is in business, thanks to Mayor Perkins, we will fund such projects. Our company is for the people. Please reelect Mayor Perkins so we can continue our fight to build a great community!"

The crowd went crazy with loud clapping and cheering as I stood there, smiling and shaking the mayor's hand.

After the rally was over, Mayor Perkins walked us to our awaiting limo and said, "Mr. Thomas, you did an amazing job up there. I think that you have just single-handedly gotten me reelected. Thank you so much. I'm forever in your debt. Remember, if you need the power of my office, don't hesitate to call."

We shook hands again, then the girls and I got into the car.

Both women gave me a hug and a kiss.

Valencia said, "This calls for a drink!" Then she poured us each a glass of champagne.

Teela said, "Baby, you've just cemented our name into the very foundation of the city. That was brilliant! Just think about when we get that bank up and running. We will own this city. We are untouchable because of the way you've played your cards."

"We will try and get as many as we can out of the hoods and into our subdivisions. Then once we have the bank up and running, we will redirect the flow of business into the subdivision's direction. We can do that by giving loans to people who will build their businesses near the subs," I said.

"Then the old hoods can remain hustling areas that won't cast a sore eye on the city because it will be out of the way of everything that's happening," added Teela.

"Drugs would be the only reason why anyone would venture that way, and getting the mayor to exclude these spots in the police's daily patrol route won't be a problem," I responded.

Valencia raised her glass for a toast and said, "Here is to plans inside of plans!"

We all burst out laughing.

When we got home, our driver opened the back door of the limo to find us all just in our underwears.

He started laughing and said, "Boss, when I grow up, I want to be just like you!"

We laughed as we danced our way inside of the house.

The next day, I was in my office when I received calls from the guys, saying that the trip went well, and we were setting up. I told them that if they wanted to fluctuate the prices, they could because we had plenty of products.

My secretary called me and said, "A young Black guy wants to talk to you about a job, sir."

I told her to let him come through.

When he walked in, I felt like something about him was so familiar. He looked really serious as he came closer.

"I understand that you're looking for work. What's your name?" I asked.

"*Chrisville Jr., mutha———ucka!*" he screamed as he upped his gun and pulled the trigger.

Fire jumped from the barrel as the deafening *boom* shattered the early-morning silence.

As I fell backward, both adjoining doors burst open simultaneously. Teela and Valencia entered, screaming, "Noooo! Please god, no!"

The End

About the Author

Jason Luv is one of the most compelling storytellers to date. The way he brings his characters to life right before your very eyes makes it hard to tell if the book is fiction or nonfiction. The story *Louisiana Slim and the Family of Dope* grips you in such a loving embrace, which is a testament to the unique set of writing skills Mr. Luv incorporates as he weaves this action-packed suspense thriller together. His perspective on life opens our minds and hearts and has us tingling for more.

Jason is a model, performer, Internet personality, and entrepreneur who has always loved writing and has now decided to share his talents with the world.

Milton Keynes UK
Ingram Content Group UK Ltd.
UKHW010241221123
432980UK00002B/244

9 798887 939964